Michael McAllister M.

A Killer's F

By Paul McNabb

All rights reserved

Copyright 2014

Cover photography by Paul McNabb

Cover graphics by GFORCE Printing & Graphics

Many thanks to Alex Tribe and Steven & Paula Power for editing

This book is dedicated to my wife, Cathy, who has shared countless adventures and ill-conceived disasters with me in our old Jag.

Facebook: Paul.McNabb.5

Chapter 1

A cold chill ran down Enrico De Costa's back the moment two men entered his office un-announced. One was a small-time local developer but the other was a tough looking stranger. The half open second drawer of his massive desk contained a loaded pistol, reserved for impolite visitors. Surprises tended to be bad for business. Without moving his upper arm he slid his right hand to the gnarled wooden handle of the forty-five, greeting his guests without rising from his chair and at the same time keeping his facial expression neutral. Reed moved forward and placed what looked like a contract on the desk but De Costa took no notice, shifting his gaze from one man to the other. Although Reed was as nervous as a cat visiting a dog pound, his partner seemed calm.

Reed started the conversation. "We were in the neighborhood and thought you might like to have a look at a new agreement for the land by the marina."

"Who's your associate, if I might ask?"

"His name is not important. Just have a look at the deal. I think you'll like it."

De Costa calmly raised the pistol, training it on the stranger. The gun barrel didn't seem to worry the new-comer much.

The stranger took control of the meeting. "I think you'll want to reconsider. May I?"

Gently opening his jacket with the thumb and fore finger of his right hand, the stranger carefully revealed the top of a cell phone in his breast pocket. With a nod toward De Costa he slowly removed the device. His thumbs made quick work of the keypad. As soon as it began to ring he stepped forward and handed it to Enrico. "It's for you."

Holding the phone to his ear De Costa heard what sounded like his wife screaming hysterically at the other end of the line.

"What in the hell is going on here?"

"We have your wife. If you sign the contracts we won't harm her."

Chapter 2

Tanya Stafford tried to control her breathing as she stood at the side of the track, bouncing lightly from one foot to the other in an attempt to remain calm. Her C-type Jaguar waited patiently on the other side for the Le Mans style start to the race. At the crack of the starter's pistol each contestant would run across the track, jump into his car and start the race as quickly as possible.

She had campaigned her Jag in the vintage series during the year, or at least most of the races, with only a second place in the final event to show for her hard work. Her team consisted of her boyfriend, Michael McAllister, possibly the most handsome man she had ever met but useless when it came to working on racing cars, Derek Hunter, a real Jag mechanic and restorer, her uncle, Peter Stafford and his friend, Buck Snider. Peter and Buck were too old to help and mainly provided moral support.

The race was being staged after the end of the regular season as a one-time tribute to the old track in Monterey. A special event had been planned and approved to run a vintage racing display to celebrate the event fifty years after the final race in 1957. Most of the old track route remained, now covered by city streets. Luckily the community of Pebble Beach liked to keep things old fashioned so the roads lacked curbs, something racing cars didn't seem to like much. Only cars that had actually competed in one of the original Monterey races were allowed to compete. Most had been discarded years ago, then resurrected from dusty barns and restored when their value shot up in the late nineties. The organizers seemed to think the race would be little more than a parade of old cars puffing through the neighborhood, belching smoke and oil and making sublime noises. Tanya had other ideas. She meant to win this race but still cursed herself for making a mistake in qualifying earlier that morning. A slide on the final turn lost valuable time, resulting in a sixth place finish out of ten cars in the time trials. One big advantage remained. Most of the owners of the expensive cars wanted to do their own driving. Most didn't run so well anymore, the result of too many good meals and glasses of fine wine. Tanya, although forty-three years old, still weighed in at a taut one hundred and ten pounds. Hopefully the hours of practicing the starting routine over the past week would pay dividends. The large steering wheel had a nasty habit of catching her foot when she hopped into the cockpit and the gear shift harbored evil intentions for a pant leg as well.

The track ran a little over two miles, beginning just north of the grand clubhouse at the Pebble Beach Golf Links. The start/finish line opened to a long straightaway running adjacent to the equestrian center, then turning right in a large U-shape for a block before returning on the far side of the manicured grassy field. Most of the spectators could see all the action along the course to this point. Four large homes had been built inside what used to be turns three, four and five. The cars disappeared around these homes and reappeared in a short straight just before the final turn leading back to the start.

Tanya took one last look at her team assembled on the far side of the track behind her car then concentrated completely on each step in the starting procedure. The noise of the crowd increased as the starter raised his pistol. At the sound of the blast she sprinted across the track in eight strides, swung gracefully into the car, hit the starter button and feathered the gas pedal. When the engine caught she shot onto the track, passing three cars before their engines came to life. Calming herself with a deep breath, she focused on the car in front of her, an Allard. What was his weakness? He had better speed but poorer handling. When they were behind the houses on the far side of the track Tanya expertly cut him off in the corner and took second place.

Now only a Ferrari Barchetta stood between her and the trophy but she trailed by several car lengths. The crowd noise rose again at the start/finish line but she zeroed in on the exhaust pipe of her adversary. Over the next three laps she steadily closed the distance. Vintage racing officials enforced one important rule: touch another car and you're disqualified. She tried to pass on the inside and outside over the next two laps, but the red blur ahead simply moved over and blocked her. On the final lap she pulled within inches of the tail of the leading car. The driver of the Ferrari struggled in the corners because his brakes were no match for the Jaguar's discs. On the final turn she waited until the

Ferrari driver braked, then faked a move inside and shot by on the outside; a dangerous maneuver at exactly the point where she had erred in the time trial. The old Jag strained for traction as it slid to the side of the road. Tanya felt like she was running on marbles but as they headed for the finish her Jaguar led by a foot. The previous owner of her car, Jack Waldorf, had raced in the 1957 event. Peter and Buck had been at the track that day and watched him win. Apparently the old Jag remembered what to do because when the official waved the checkered flag she was still ahead by a nose.

* * *

Michael nursed a serious hang-over when he and Tanya gingerly descended the stairs around noon the next day. The big idea to invite the other teams over for a few drinks turned out to be quite a challenge. Everyone in the racing community wanted to see the old Waldorf mansion in Los Gatos that Tanya had been renovating over the past year and who was going to refuse free drinks? The last guests had departed well after two in the morning. Peter, Buck, and Derek had been too drunk to drive so Tanya forced them to sleep over. Only the smell of bacon and eggs managed to rouse them. After a hearty meal the team walked to the racing garage located down the hill a hundred yards behind the main house.

"You know I was at the race fifty years ago when Jack won. He pulled the very same maneuver in the final turn, passing on the outside and holding on 'til the finish. The same Ferrari was involved in the scuffle, too."

"That's about the tenth time you've told us that story, Peter. I was pretty sure I could get by him on the last corner. I noticed the Ferrari team hadn't really redone the brakes very well. I was just worried I might spin out."

Michael asked, "If you knew it was going to be risky, why did you try it?"

"I figured a few years from now no one would remember who finished second so I just went for the win."

Buck piped in, "I thought I was going to have a heart attack. Jack's old C-type is a blue blood for sure. Once she got ahead she wasn't going to give up the lead."

The car was filthy but the team decided to leave the grit for a while, allowing the feeling of the race to linger. Buck's attention waned suddenly during a conversation with Michael, as he stared over his shoulder toward the door with his mouth agape. When Michael turned to see what had captured Buck's gaze, he immediately imitated Buck's behavior. A young man stood in the open door, his gaze fixed on the mural painted across the back wall. The blond imposing figure was a dead ringer for Jack Waldorf. Two young bodyguards, who had the look of men who could take care of themselves, stood at his side. Both were dark skinned with jet black hair, Italian looking. Matching bulges under their respective jackets sent a message they meant business. Michael realized someone needed to say something.

"May we help you?"

Buck turned his gaze to Michael.

"You can see him, too?"

The stranger ignored his comment.

"My name is Valentino De Costa. My parents are missing. I need your help."

Chapter 3

"Let's head back to the house. We can have something cool to drink while you fill us in."

Michael remembered a strange tale Buck had spun a year earlier about seeing Jack Waldorf around town from time to time which was pretty amazing since he'd been dead for forty-five plus years. Buck must have thought old age was playing tricks on him but it turned out a young man closely resembling Jack actually lived in the area. Michael urged Buck to head home when he calmed down. Peter and Derek realized Michael might have some business to discuss so they departed as well.

Michael used the one hundred yard walk back to the main house to carefully observe De Costa, a dashing figure at over six feet tall, muscular, blond hair with blue eyes and bearing the same features as Jack Waldorf, the original owner of the mansion they now inhabited. His purposeful stride, along with the elegant manner in which he carried himself, commanded respect. Michael caught Tanya staring at him, something rare because she'd seen plenty of pretty boys in her day. Sure he was handsome, he'd give her that, but there was something almost regal about him. His voice sang in a forceful baritone. The matching bodyguards followed closely behind, constantly combing the surroundings for anyone who might exhibit the poor judgment to threaten the boss.

"Valentino, how did you know to walk down to the racing garage when you couldn't find anyone at the main house?"

The question seemed fair. Everyone except the five from the racing crew had gone home the night before. The road from the back of the main house curved gracefully around the trees, preventing a direct view. How did he know about the racing garage? Questions like this demanded answers in McAllister's book.

"I had a strange feeling I'd been here before. I can't place it but it seemed like someone brought me here when I was a very small child. I remember walking down a path lined with flowers of many hues casting an eerie scene, almost like a dream. When I came to the main house I just seemed to know the road led to a garage down here."

The answer seemed odd but Michael filed it away for further analysis. The beauty of the mansion impressed as it came into view through the trees. A screened porch had originally stretched across the entire back of the residence with gigantic Bougainvillea vines covering it. The redesigned house matched the garage in Tuscan stucco with a faux tile roof but full-length windows now covered the back of the house, offering a brighter and more inviting look. A pool curved under the windows with a hot tub on one end and a koi pond on the other. Large flat stones formed a patio with fine manicured grass standing at attention in between.

Michael gestured toward chairs by the pool while Tanya disappeared into the kitchen. A hummingbird darted in his face for an instant, possibly attracted by his blue baseball cap and then disappeared. The bodyguards refused refreshments. Standing at attention near the house, they politely refused the offer to sit as well. Michael began the detective work as soon as Tanya returned. He wasn't a man to waste words.

"Why me?"

"When you killed the Slasher in Saratoga last year the news made headlines around here for weeks. I did a search on the computer, too. You've been involved in some big cases. I heard you two had purchased the old Waldorf mansion so you were easy to find."

"I'm afraid I don't do detective work anymore. The Slasher case was a fluke."

"I'm in big trouble. I need your help."

Michael glanced over at Tanya. She returned a look that made it clear she wanted him to help. "Okay, Valentino. I guess I can at least listen to what you have to say but I don't think I'm going to be much good to you."

"Please call me Blue, as all my friends do." He seemed to compose himself for a moment before beginning his story. "My parents are Denise and Enrico De Costa. They've been missing five days. The last time I saw my dad was Wednesday at work. I left early in the afternoon because I had plans with friends in San

11

Jose for the evening. I returned home quite late, probably three or so in the morning. I showered around seven and dressed for work but when I came upstairs the kitchen was empty. I was surprised because my mother always made breakfast. Only after I searched upstairs did I realize they were missing. Their bed had not been used so I'm sure they disappeared sometime the previous evening.

"I work for my father. Our family owns substantial real estate holdings in Monterey. Our office is located there, as well. I ride with him to work every morning, allowing him to advise me on all the projects in progress. He's training me to take over the family business." Blue paused and looked directly and forcefully into Michael's eyes. "There is no way on earth my parents would have left town without advising me."

"You say when you returned home you found your parents missing. You live at the same residence?"

"Yes, I occupy an apartment downstairs."

McAllister found a man of Blue's age living at home odd, another piece of information to be considered more closely when time allowed. "The police should be involved. Surely you've contacted them?"

"I did Thursday morning. They cooperated completely at first. A missing persons report was filled out immediately. I guess I pushed too hard, though. My relationship with the chief quickly deteriorated. I visited the station so many times during the next two days I was banned from the premises. The police claimed they couldn't get any work done. My worry is the chief is in way over his head on this case. Most of the crime in Los Gatos consists of graffiti and stolen bicycles. I don't think he's made any headway."

Michael was surprised Tanya had managed to stay out of the conversation.

"Nothing's happened like this before? No last minute trips or anything?"

"There is, quite simply, no business I don't know about. I have only one lead. We own a ranch in the foothills of the Santa Cruz Mountains. We built a nice modern lodge to entertain clients from time to time. My father always drives an old Chevy pick-up truck, light blue with a white top, when he visits up there. I think it's a fifties model or something. I tried to get him to buy a new one but he loves the old thing. His city car, a new Ferrari, is parked in the garage at our residence. The truck is missing. I think he drove to the ranch."

"Why didn't you just go up there and look for him?"

"I did but I couldn't find anything. The ranch is over ten thousand acres."

The last piece of information caught McAllister off guard. "I think we need to start over. Can you describe the business you and your father own in a little more detail?"

The ex-detective studied De Costa carefully as he answered questions, watching for signs of nervousness. His demeanor remained calm, never showing any hesitation while providing clear and concise answers. Michael judged he was telling the truth.

"I'm a third generation American. My grand-father, Mario, emigrated from Italy. The only profession he knew in the old country was growing olives. When he arrived in California he managed to leverage his meager savings for some cheap land north of here suitable for an orchard. He schooled his son, Enrico, in the family business. It's our way. Mario and Enrico prospered and bought more land adjacent to the first orchard. After World War Two Stanford University decided to lease land they owned near the campus to encourage highly technical companies to locate nearby so they could collaborate with research. Our olive groves happened to be just south of the Stanford properties. Enrico's training changed from learning the olive business to selling our land to developers.

"The two of them spent the next twenty-odd years selling the land. My father learned quickly the slower he sold, the more money he got for the parcels. When they sold off the last of the land, Mario and Enrico moved the family business to Monterey. Enrico built his home in Los Gatos because he liked the slower pace of living compared to Monterey."

California had been Michael's home for only a little over a year. Tanya seemed to sense he was still in the dark so she made it crystal clear.

"Your olive groves were located right in the middle of what became Silicon Valley."

"Yes. I followed in my father's footsteps. He decided I should attend San Jose State University to pursue a degree in business. I've ridden to work with my father just about every day since I graduated. We invested the money from Silicon Valley into real estate, mainly in the city of Monterey. We own many properties along the bay. Most of the real estate parcels have been developed but a few are still waiting for the right project."

"Tell me more about the ranch."

"It's in our blood to hunt. Again, the land in the hills was cheap when Mario and Enrico bought it; thought by others to be worthless."

"Okay. This is starting to make a little sense now. It would seem like the local police would go to the Monterey police or at least Santa Cruz for help. One of the departments must own a helicopter. Using a chopper would be the only way to do a proper search of an area that large."

"Believe it or not even Monterey doesn't own a helicopter. If the local police asked for help they'd undoubtedly be able to find a helicopter but at this point I don't want any other police departments involved." Michael was confused but he decided to give Blue a chance to explain himself. "I would prefer to try to control the situation myself. My father always enjoyed a good relationship with the locals. He made a lot of charitable contributions here in Los Gatos. Even though I've been banned from the station I still trust the chief. Monterey and Santa Cruz are a different story. We have enemies there. I want to keep them out of this if I can. I want to hire you to help the police in Los Gatos. I'm sure I can influence them to cooperate with you."

"I was a detective for twenty years in Tulsa but I've been retired for a couple of years now. I'm not certified or bonded in California to do any type of investigations. I'm not in a position to do any client work."

"You found the Slasher when no one else could and killed him with your own hands. I'm asking you to help me find my parents. I want to hire you. Money is no object."

Tanya decided to help Michael make up his mind on the matter.

"Of course we'll help you. We'll find them, somehow, no matter what it takes."

A raised eyebrow slyly checked Michael's reaction although she appeared pretty sure of the result. The detective business had come calling again and Michael immediately sensed a feeling of foreboding. Tanya seemed inclined to ignore what a bad idea it was to get involved in another case. After a brief pause he accepted his fate.

"Let's get something straight. I don't want to work for you. I'll look into this, but only as a favor. If I don't like what I find, I'm out."

"I'll call the police chief and tell him to do whatever you say."

"The local cops won't think much of you pushing me on them and they aren't obligated to cooperate with you, anyway. Let me go down to the station in the morning and introduce myself. I'll let them know I'm trying to help. Find a private helicopter so we can do a proper search of the ranch tomorrow. Don't be too polite when you call around because we've already lost a lot of precious time. We need to determine without any doubt whether or not a crime was committed at the ranch and we need to know immediately."

"I have to stop by the office first thing in the morning. We have several projects on the go so I'll have to get everybody lined out for the day. It'll probably take me some time to find a helicopter, too. Give me your cell number. I'll try to be ready around lunch time. Do you want some names at the police station?"

"That won't be necessary. I know what to do."

Chapter 4

A three car garage attached to the main house at the old Waldorf estate stored the cars used for daily driving. Tanya sped away early the next morning in her modern Jaguar for a meeting in San Francisco. Michael fired up Lucille, his 1960 Jaguar XK150, for the trip downtown. The old Jag remained his only car even though he'd moved from Oklahoma to California over a year before. When the idle dropped, a sign the car had warmed up, he backed into the bright sunlight.

Tanya provided directions to the police station, knowledge hopefully gained from filing permits with the city rather than doing time. A sign over a two story building announced Los Gatos/Monte Sereno Police Department a few minutes later. El Sereno Mountain rose almost two thousand feet above sea level near the Waldorf place. The municipality consisted of a few thousand people. Michael wasn't sure where it ended and Los Gatos began. Apparently the cities shared a police department. Maybe Blue was right; the case might be too big for the locals to handle. Finding a parking spot near the main entrance was easy. The detective risked leaving the Jag with the top down during his visit. A finely manicured lawn bordered the walk to the front door. The Los Gatos police seemed to have plenty of time to keep the grass trimmed.

Michael asked for the Police Chief, a man he found out was named Sean Palatine. The name sounded Irish. When he entered his office he noticed Palatine was size triple X; not particularly over weight, just a very large man with freckled white skin topped with a big mop of red hair. The detective business told him the chief was mid-forties. A catcher's mitt posing as a hand caused Michael's to disappear when they shook. The chief applied a decent crush to let him know who was boss.

"Michael McAllister. I'm going to have to tell my wife I got visited by a superstar detective today. I heard you and your girlfriend were rebuilding the Waldorf place. I thought I might bump into you eventually. What can I do for you?"

Michael remembered seeing him at the Slasher crime scene on the night he had to fight to the death with the serial killer. A gang of police officers had surrounded him at the scene that night but the chief stood out. It occurred to McAllister that Palatine might have even been in charge of the crime scene investigation. The detective wasn't sure if Saratoga had its own police department.

"I've gotten myself tangled up in something. I'm pretty sure you're not going to like it."

The chief's expression changed from friendly to serious.

"Try me."

"Valentino De Costa."

The chief's face grew sterner. "Keep talking."

"Blue came up to the house yesterday. He wanted to hire me."

"He doesn't think we can handle the investigation?"

"I think he feels helpless."

"What does he think you can do for him that we can't? I thought I read in the paper you were a writer or something now."

"Exactly what I told him. I was a detective in Tulsa in an earlier life but since then I've been pretending to earn a living writing articles about classic automobiles. I guess Blue would like to hire every private eye in the state on the chance one might help him find out what happened to his parents. It seems like he could afford it."

"Do you have any credentials in California?"

"No."

"Carry a gun?"

"I have two with me but I don't carry them on a day to day basis."

"What do you plan to do?"

"I asked Blue to hire a helicopter so we can conduct a proper search of the ranch. In my opinion eliminating the ranch should be the first step in the investigation."

"Why the ranch?"

"Blue said his dad owns an old truck that's missing. Apparently the only time he used it was when he visited the ranch."

"Same conclusion I came to. I sent an officer up there the first day to look around."

"Did he find anything?"

"It's a big ranch. I like the helicopter idea. One thing, though."

McAllister tried to form an intelligent yet quizzed expression. The chief took a card from a wooden holder on his desk. He wrote a number on it and slid it across the desk.

"This is my direct cell number. If you find anything call me immediately. I don't want you disturbing any evidence. You should be familiar with proper police procedures." The chief seemed to be having a little trouble controlling his anger. "I might as well make it plain to you, I'm not happy about this. De Costa thinks he owns the police department for some reason. He's been in charge of the family business for a few days and he's ready to start calling the shots for the whole town. I don't need a bunch of half-wits getting in my way. This case is going to be tough enough as it is. You've got a bit of a reputation, too, for taking matters into your own hands. I'm not saying I wasn't happy you got the Slasher, but I don't want a repeat of you killing someone in my jurisdiction."

"Since we're getting to be best friends and speaking frankly, get this straight: I'm not working for Blue. I only agreed to try to help. I think after a day of searching he'll move on to someone else. I'm not going to get in your way on this case." Palatine gave him a respectful nod so the detective continued. "Do you have any ideas about the disappearance of his parents?"

"We won't find them alive. If they had been kidnapped we would have received a demand for some serious money by now. They're a very close family. No way Enrico wouldn't be communicating with his son if he was alive."

"Is Blue a suspect?"

"Everybody's a suspect, as a detective you know that. Blue's been a pain in the ass from the first day but personally I don't think he's involved. We know he was partying with some friends up in San Jose the night his parents went missing. He's got a group of buddies from his college days he visits on a regular basis. We tracked down a few witnesses to confirm his story. The time line for him being involved won't work. He was too far away. His alibi is rock solid as far as I'm concerned. He doesn't have a motive, either. He's an only child. He knows he's going to get everything. Why would he knock off his parents? Blue's involvement in the murders doesn't make sense.

"The De Costa family is well thought of in this town. His father was supportive when I ran for police chief. They're involved in the community; very generous if you know what I mean. I'd do anything to help them. However, it's not the same in Monterey. I heard about some trouble his father had over there recently." Pausing for a moment, the chief looked McAllister over from across the desk. "I'm sure this will lead back to the family business at some point but I'm trying to keep the other police departments out of the investigation until I have a chance to look around. I don't know how much longer I can stall if I don't come up with something. The county already wants to take over the case out of Salinas. Monterey's trying to claim jurisdiction, too, because of the office. The helicopter could be a big help."

"Okay. Tomorrow we'll perform a proper search from the air. If something turns up, you'll be the first person I call."

The catcher's mitt appeared again as McAllister prepared to leave but this time the chief didn't let go. Instead he offered a final piece of information. "Two things. First, I'm beholden to the De Costa family. Like I said, the old man helped me get elected chief. Since we're trying to start with a clean slate I want you to understand something. I won't break the law for Blue. I'll put everything I have into the investigation but I won't be his henchman."

"I wouldn't either. What else?"

"Before you leave give my admin your social security number and some references back in Tulsa. I'm going to check you out properly."

Paperwork, not McAllister's favorite pastime, delayed his departure a few minutes. On the way home his cell phone rang, showing the name Valentino De Costa on the call display.

"I should be at your place by lunch."

Chapter 5

A bright blue helicopter dropped gracefully to a small clearing on the lawn behind the pool just after one. Tanya cut the morning meetings short because she had designated herself Michael's partner in the investigation. They climbed into the back seats while Blue, sans body guards, remained in front beside the pilot. Michael was a little uneasy in the chopper for no particular reason other than they didn't seem to glide very well; but he was reassured by the ultra-cleanliness of the craft, seemingly brand new. The machine made quite a racket but as soon as they fastened their seat belts they donned headphones with microphones on the end of a small metal bar made of chrome. Communicating through this system proved a little disorienting.

Once airborne a crackle from the pilot informed them, "We'll touch down at the ranch in about twenty minutes."

The pilot found plenty of room to land near the lodge when they arrived. He found plenty of room, period. The bodyguard question was answered by two huge trucks that had transported what looked to be ten or so heavily armed men now stationed around the property. Michael guessed Blue wasn't taking any chances with another attempt on his family. What De Costa called a ranch house would have been better described as a medium-sized hotel done in a rustic log cabin style. Six bedrooms, each with its own en suite, occupied the second level. A large outdoor kitchen allowed clients to enjoy a panoramic view of the ocean forty miles in the distance from an elevation of three thousand feet. A grand hunting party with booze flowing freely and a wild boar roasting on an open fire wasn't hard to imagine. A half hour nosing around the large cabin yielded no sign of forced entry or any use of the facility. Blue described the premises just as it had been when locked after the last time he and his father had entertained clients some weeks back.

Blue gave Michael a quizzed look. "Now what?"

"Let's use the chopper to follow the dirt roads around the property. We'll have four sets of eyes looking for anything out of the ordinary."

The small army remained at the lodge while the others re-boarded the chopper. Only a few roads snaked through the ranch making a systematic search tricky but do-able. The landscape rolled lazily through hills and ravines for the most part but a few areas dropped off dramatically, falling to a large stream cutting through the property. Occasionally bodies of water appeared; mostly something between large ponds and small lakes as far as McAllister was concerned. After forty-five minutes the pilot warned he had to keep a close eye on his fuel. Ten minutes later they flew over one of the larger bodies of water. Three of them missed it but not Tanya. She screamed and gestured as she slapped the pilot on the back.

"Turn around. Go back where the road turns at the end of the water."

The helicopter performed a lazy turn and flew back where they first crossed the water. The white roof of the blue truck was clearly visible a few feet below the surface. Blue immediately took charge.

"Land down by the road!"

He leapt from the chopper before the rotors had stopped turning and raced to the edge of the water, murky from a recent rain. The reflection of light off the surface hid the truck from view, at least from the bank. Blue started to unbutton his shirt.

"What are you doing?" Michael's mind was racing for something to say to keep him out of the water. Even underwater the truck could hold clues to the identity of the killer.

"I'm going to find out if my parents are in the truck."

"You can't do that."

"The hell I can't."

"This is a crime scene. It must be investigated properly."

"I'm going in and no one's going to stop me."

"Then you better take this."

When he turned McAllister landed a hard right on his chin, dropping Blue to the ground; apparently something that didn't happen to him often. Tanya knelt beside him as he tried to regain his senses. When he'd recovered a bit from the shock of being socked, Michael tried to reason with him again.

"We're all pretty sure your parents are in that truck. I've investigated more than my share of murders. I don't want you to remember them this way. I'm begging you to take the chopper back to the lodge. Tanya, I'd like you to go with him. I'll wait here until the police arrive. I'll call you on your cell phone when we know something."

Blue grudgingly agreed, not verbally, but by looking at the pilot and motioning to the helicopter. Tanya was a different matter.

"I'm warning you; this is going to be bad. You'll be sorry if you stick around."

"I stay with you. That's my rule."

Michael flipped open his cell phone and was relieved to find a weak but usable signal. He didn't waste time when Palatine answered.

"We found the truck in a body of water at the ranch. You'll need divers to investigate the crime scene and a tow truck to get it out. I don't know how to explain our exact location."

"What about the helicopter?"

"I had the pilot take Blue back to the lodge at the main gate. I don't want him to see what's inside the truck."

"Who else is with you?"

"Just Tanya but Blue has some men at the main house."

"I'll be there in an hour. Keep Blue's men away from the crime scene."

After finding a large rock to use as a sofa, Michael and Tanya found plenty of time to talk while they waited for the authorities.

"My advice is to turn your back when the truck comes out of the water." He gave her a hug and rubbed her back. "I wish we hadn't gotten involved in this."

"I just wanted to help Blue. I see what you mean, though. Real police work isn't nearly as glamorous as I thought it would be."

"It's going to get cold, too, when the suns goes down. Usually at times like this it starts raining."

The grinding of a motor told them a truck was approaching before they saw it. Five or six of Blue's men were visible when the truck rounded a corner and charged toward the crime scene. McAllister ran with his arms extended to stop them well before they reached the area showing tire marks entering the water. Taking impressions of all the tread marks might be crucial in solving the case. He positioned the men in a broad arc a safe distance from any potential evidence. Palatine was good on his word, arriving in a little over an hour with another truck full of investigators and a tow truck bringing up the rear. A diver performed a preliminary investigation of the scene underwater, checking for evidence in a ten foot perimeter. Later the winch groaned on the tow truck, grudgingly revealing the blue and white truck. Enrico was clearly visible bent over the steering wheel as water gushed from the open door on his side of the truck. A shape next to him was more difficult to ascertain until the detective realized the head was dangling from what was left of a spinal cord. The flesh on both corpses was grotesquely swollen and deformed. Tanya convulsed when she realized what she was seeing, causing her to turn and walk away. Large matching holes on each side of the windshield told McAllister the De Costas had been shot with a shotgun at close range. Their bodies were intact but Enrico's head was shredded past the point of recognition. Apparently the kill shot to his wife hit in the neck area. Turtles and catfish might have been working on the exposed flesh, as well.

"Michael. Over here." The chief nodded toward a spot a short distance away from the scene. "This is how it's going to be. You and Tanya were never here. One of my officers was continuing the investigation and found the truck. You have a problem with that?"

"I don't but what about Blue and his men?"

"My story will be I called Blue when I got the report and told him to meet me up here."

The chief paused to let Michael take in the information. "I have to call the sheriff in Salinas now that we found the truck in their jurisdiction. I'm sure they'll take the truck and the corpses to the county facilities for investigation. If I bring them in now, we'll get better cooperation. Are you sure we're good on this?"

"Yeah, we're good. I just have to figure out a way to get Tanya and I home."

"I'll get you two a ride back up to the lodge with Blue's men. I don't want them down here at the scene when the sheriff shows up. Blue will have to figure out how to get you home."

Michael told Tanya the story while Palatine rounded up Blue's men. The whole group rode silently in two trucks over a crude road back to the lodge. Michael dreaded a face to face meeting with Blue but he knew what had to be done; drawing him away from the others so they could talk privately.

"Take a deep breath. I'm going to give it to you like a man." Blue nodded but his face said he was lying. "Your parents were in the truck. Both had been shot at close range through the windshield with a shotgun." Michael put a hand on Blue's shoulder and gripped firmly. "At least they didn't suffer." He let the news soak in for a moment before he continued. "There's a catch, though. Palatine wants to take credit for finding the truck." Blue's face quickly contorted in anger. "Before you blow up, think it through. I think it's a good break for us." Blue's face changed to incredulous. "We give him the credit and he scores big points in the media but he owes you one. You might need some favors later." Blue nodded his agreement to the plan.

"What about me and my men?"

"The story is he called you on your cell phone when he confirmed he'd found your parents."

"What about you and Tanya?"

"I suggest you fly us back home in the chopper. We were never here. I'd give the pilot a couple of hundred bucks to keep his mouth shut if I were you. Palatine's calling the sheriff in Salinas so you better get the story straight with your men and make sure they don't mess up."

When Tanya and Michael arrived home he poured them each a glass of wine before they headed upstairs. She never spoke about what they had seen but pulled Michael's arms around her tightly when they were under the covers. Murders were the ultimate reality.

Chapter 6

As was his custom, he parked over a mile from the Waldorf house then walked along back streets through a couple of neighborhoods to get closer. As dusk set in he made the final half mile through the woods using a deer trail he now knew by heart. The creek was low, allowing him to cross using some stepping stones as cars roared over the bridge just to his right. An hour later he sat motionless in the woods observing the back of the mansion while he considered the situation carefully. He'd checked through a window on the side of the garage and found both of their cars inside but his prey didn't seem to be home. The facts didn't make sense. During the last few months he'd tracked them meticulously. They followed their habits predictably. A new wrinkle at this late date could destroy his whole plan.

He considered a quick search of the house but just then a helicopter approached, directing a tunnel of light towards the back lawn. Seconds after landing Michael and Tanya disembarked and the helicopter slowly rose and disappeared into the night.

Quite an entrance. He followed their movements through the large windows as lights illuminated the kitchen. After a few minutes the first floor grew dark again and the lights upstairs appeared. He wondered if they would have sex. Probably so. They usually did. The upstairs went dark after only a few minutes.

The night was cool. Sitting motionless he listened for animals. Deer walked remarkably close by, keeping an eye on him as they passed. The cloudless sky showed a million stars twinkling brightly. After a full hour he finally judged it safe and approached the back of the house by the pool. The lock on the door quickly surrendered to his tools. He held his breath as he entered. He pulled the door almost but not quite shut, allowing for a quick getaway if needed. After a moment his eyes adjusted to the total darkness, allowing him to ascend the stairs.

Carefully controlling his breathing, he pulled a pistol from his jacket pocket. Tanya's back was cuddled up against Michael spoon-style. Both seemed to be in a deep sleep. As he stepped to the side of the bed, the intruder held the gun inches from Michael's temple and moved his finger to the trigger. *Too easy.* He backed out of the room but continued to point the gun at Michael. The final dress rehearsal went exactly as planned. The next time would be for real.

Chapter 7

Chief Palatine jingled McAllister on his cell phone early the next afternoon.

"You have anything important planned for this evening?"

"That depends on what you have in mind."

"I'd like you to come to the station around seven. I know it's not much warning. I'll understand if you can't make it."

Tanya shot him an inquiring stare as he spoke on the phone. "Just me?"

"Just you."

"Okay, seven."

"Park your old jalopy in the back by the patrol cars this time. It wouldn't look good if somebody stole it from in front of the police station."

Michael wondered what the chief could be up to. Tanya gave him the silent treatment until he left. He knew he'd better return home with a story considerably more complete than a mere police report. Lucille found a comfortable spot inside the fenced lot as ordered and McAllister entered through the back of the station. The musty smell of every police station in the world filled his nostrils, although he thought the Beverly Hills station might be different. A couple of officers milling around gave him a stare as if Tanya was having him tailed.

"I'm looking for the chief."

"Down the hall and to the right."

The chief seemed like he was watching for McAllister because he was looking into a room but standing in the hall so he could see the detective when he approached. The chief motioned the other way. When they were seated in his office Palatine began a seemingly prepared speech.

"I called Tulsa. The chief said you were the best detective the department ever had."

"They're just hoping you'll give me a job so I won't come back."

"I might just make you an offer but right now I'm dealing with something else. I think I might have screwed up." McAllister gave him a look that asked for more information. "We did a preliminary search of the De Costa house when Blue's parents first went missing. Nothing seemed out of order at the time but the crime scene at the ranch kind of changed things. I think I might have missed something at the house. I asked Blue to leave so we could have one more go at his place. The sheriff will be down here in no time. I want to go over everything one more time before he takes over."

"What's this got to do with me?"

"You've investigated a lot of murder scenes, right?"

"I guess you could say that. Certainly all the serial killer scenes back home. I guess plenty of others, too."

"We haven't investigated a murder here in five years. I don't count the Slasher case because every police officer in northern

California horned in on that one. We had a murder here the first year I was chief but it was cut and dried; a woman shot her husband then drove to the station and confessed. What I'm saying is we haven't done this very often. I don't want to make a mistake. I've got a crime scene technician who's only a few years out of school. Her dad was the chief before me but got himself killed in a car wreck. She put herself through college with the insurance money. She's putting a lot of pressure on herself with the De Costa case."

"What exactly do you want me to do?"

"I want you to tag along and watch over our shoulders. You're not associated with any police force so if we start to screw up maybe you could say something."

"Tell me about the first investigation on the house."

"Like I said, it was a preliminary search. We looked for signs of a struggle but didn't find anything that seemed out of place. We took a lot of fingerprints. Nothing's come of that so far. The only set of rogue prints turned out to be from one of my dumbass cops. I gave strict instructions to wear gloves but Wilson managed to contaminate some areas in the kitchen. We found a fair amount of money in a safe. Makes me think robbery wasn't a motive. Now that we know the truck was definitely involved I think maybe the house was where this whole thing started. We're going back tonight to look for blood. My tech wanted me to do it the first time but I said no. I guess that makes me a dumbass, too."

"I didn't actually conduct any tests at the crime scenes but I watched the experts do it. I just tried to make sense of the results."

"Just watch what we're doing. Speak up if we seem like we're missing something." McAllister got up from his chair. "One more thing." McAllister waited for the one more thing.

"My tech's going to freak out when she realizes what you're doing. You're like a superstar detective. She might not recognize your face but she'll know your name when I introduce you."

"I'll handle it."

"I appreciate this. Finding the truck was a huge break for us. This could be a big help, too." They headed back to the room Palatine was looking into when McAllister arrived. Inside a table was covered with cans of luminol clearly marked as such along with a couple of other stray bottles he didn't recognize. A young woman, who McAllister judged to be in her late twenties, was boxing supplies for the trip. She seemed startled to see the chief with a stranger. "Stacy Carson, meet Michael McAllister. He's going with us tonight."

The realization that someone was going to be looking over her shoulder flashed across her face almost instantly. She was the epitome of a police officer, trim and fit, with luxurious brown hair high-lighted in gold; cut short but manicured better than the lawn out front. If she gobbled a couple of super-sized meals she might have weighed a hundred pounds.

"Officer Carson, it's a pleasure to meet you." Michael's hand was attacked with the most ferocious grip he'd ever encountered from a woman. Obviously she wanted to be treated as a professional. "I want to make it clear I am only here as an interdepartmental courtesy. You are in complete charge of this investigation. I will follow your orders explicitly."

He didn't elaborate on which department he was actually representing because one didn't exist. The color came back to her face as she nodded slightly. As she loaded the chief's truck, an Expedition, McAllister offered to help carry the testing supplies but Carson would have none of it. A sheepish Officer Wilson greeted the threesome when they arrived at the De Costa residence, obviously still in Palatine's doghouse. The officer had been assigned the job of guarding the potential crime scene to make sure no one entered. Palatine ordered him to unlock the doors and open the garage then turned to Carson.

"Where do we start?"

She was way ahead of him. "The truck was obviously involved. Blue told us it was parked in the middle of the other two cars. That's the obvious place to start. I'll mix up a batch of spray so we can get moving." She folded down the trunk lid of the chief's truck to use as a table. The well-lit garage offered an open parking spot for investigation. "McAllister, climb up on that stool and unscrew the light. I've got to close the garage door." Carson seemed to be taking the control thing a little over the top. Palatine began an eerie conversation in the near pitch dark room, filling McAllister in on the potential crime scene as Carson began testing areas of the garage.

"Two things I want to mention about the house. First, old man De Costa had a large safe in the floor of the basement, located down the hall from that door over there." The chief gestured to the only door to the house from the garage, barely visible as the detective's eyes began to adjust to the darkness. "Blue had a difficult time locating the combination but he finally managed to open it. We found just short of twenty thousand dollars in cash along with a few pieces of pretty serious jewelry and some business papers."

McAllister speculated. "Maybe whoever did this couldn't force De Costa to open the safe."

"Same conclusion I came to. We also found a large gun safe in the basement. De Costa was a collector because the lock up contained about twenty shotguns and a few pistols. So far only one gun is missing, a small two shot derringer-like gun belonging to Denise."

"Mrs. De Costa carried a gun?"

"Always. Blue said she even had it in her apron when she washed the dishes."

"Why would she bother carrying a gun when they have a small army of security with them all the time?"

"The crew following Blue everywhere he goes is new. Old man De Costa handled everything himself. Blue hired the small army, as you call it, right after his parents disappeared."

"You haven't found her gun?"

"No. It wasn't on the body or in the truck."

"Bingo." Their conversation was interrupted by Carson. "Several hits over here by the door. I've got to get my camera. I'm going to take some pictures and then a video."

Michael performed tasks as ordered over the next two hours as Stacy worked her way inside the house, up the stairs and finally to the kitchen. Generally his duties consisted of holding the black light source when she needed to take photographs or video. After each photo session she collected samples. Palatine and McAllister took care not to get in her way. Michael flipped the light off in the kitchen at her command after she'd sprayed the floor. A two foot circle glowed in the middle of the floor, eerily shining in electric blue. Someone had obviously been hurt there, too badly to have survived in Michael's opinion. It seemed obvious a body had been taken out of the kitchen, across the living room, down the stairs and out to the garage.

On the way back to the station Michael decided to earn his fee with a comment from the back seat. "The evidence doesn't make sense."

"Explain yourself." The chief replied. Carson turned sideways so she could look at the detective between the bucket seats.

"The De Costas weren't shot in the kitchen because a shot gun blast would have made a terrible mess. Still, it appears one of them died at the house. Did you find any stab wounds on the bodies?"

"From my brief conversation with the sheriff this morning no wounds were found on the victims other than one shotgun blast each from close range."

"Maybe the derringer was used on one of them. You might have to ask the coroner to look for a small bullet in the head of one of the victims. A wound like that would be easy to miss with the deterioration of the bodies. It might also explain why the small gun is missing. At least DNA testing will tell you which one of them was murdered in the kitchen. How long will it take you to get the test results?"

Palatine's face contorted in the rear view mirror.

"At least a month if we're lucky. Do you have any pull with the state crime lab?"

Carson must have been saving up her energy on the drive back because she punished McAllister's hand even more when she shook it as he prepared to leave. "Would you mind giving me your cell number? I'd like to discuss some of your cases when this blows over."

She quickly entered his name and number in her cell. He made one last effort to make sure she was on his side.

"By the way, you handled yourself as a true professional back there. You didn't need my help for anything."

She was still glowing when he fired up Lucille, arriving home around midnight. Unfortunately Tanya's interrogation lasted well over an hour. She demanded every detail of the evening including the color of Carson's hair and eyes and her approximate weight and build.

Chapter 8

It figured Valentino De Costa would be overwhelmed by the arrangements for a double funeral over the next week. The chief didn't seem to feel obligated to keep Michael updated on the case, either. The detective allowed himself to dream his involvement was over. The murders weren't the ending Blue had hoped for but at least he'd found his parents.

A gentleman in Palo Alto, who owned the first E-type Jaguar delivered to California in the early sixties, offered a welcome distraction from the case, allowing McAllister to meet yet another deadline for his monthly column in the classic Jaguar magazine. Scanned pictures of the car when it was originally purchased high-lighted the story. The owner had even proposed to his future wife in the car. A light restoration, consisting mainly of a paint job, had recently been performed because the car was in such original condition. The finished product could have passed for a brand new car as delivered fifty-some years earlier; just the kind of story the readers loved. As he finished e-mailing the text and pictures from his laptop, McAllister found out he was wrong about Blue. When he answered the ring of his cell phone, De Costa asked for a lunch meeting the following day.

Michael and Tanya met him at the Los Gatos Bar & Grill, a sports bar where locals could enjoy a good burger and watch a ball game. McAllister stood as De Costa entered the restaurant. His eyes looked older than when they'd met a few days earlier.

Two new guards remained by the door, interchangeable with the others, dark skinned with jet black hair. Matching bulges under their jackets signaled they were ready for trouble. McAllister wondered if anyone else in the restaurant noticed they were carrying guns. The detective prepared to take his medicine.

"If you want to deck me, I've got it coming."

Blue managed a weak smile and motioned for him to sit down. "You did the right thing but I'm afraid I have another favor to ask."

"I'm listening."

"You found my parents but I want to know who killed them. The crime scene at the ranch makes no sense as far as I'm concerned."

"What have the police told you since the last time we saw you?"

"Nothing of substance. I heard the truck is getting the full treatment in Salinas but they haven't found anything new. The authorities allowed me back in my house so I assume they don't think they're going to find any more evidence. The sheriff's crew did a job on the place after Palatine finished. You know about the blood in the kitchen."

McAllister stared at him a second before he spoke again. "Blue, you've got to understand there's not a lot more I can do for you."

"You found the truck in one day. I'm asking for anything."

When Michael looked over to Tanya he got a stare that said she'd already formed an opinion on the involvement matter. Her expression said it would be a good idea to agree.

"Maybe we should have a chat with Chief Palatine. He seems pretty straight to me. I think he wants to help you. Let's see what he'll tell us."

"When?"

Michael looked over at Tanya. "I guess I'll ride with you, Blue. The station's pretty close. Tanya, you can head back to the house."

"Like hell I will. We'll follow Blue over to the station."

She gave him her evil smile knowing he could never say no to her. Blue waited while they finished their lunch. McAllister used the opportunity to ask a few more questions.

"Tell me about the safe at the house."

"What about it?"

"Did your father routinely keep a lot of money in it?"

"He didn't feel the need to share information about what he kept in the safe with me."

"You didn't keep anything in the safe?"

"I don't own anything valuable enough to keep in a safe. I happened to see him put the combination in a book he keeps near his desk. I was lucky to open it for the police the other night. It held about twenty thousand dollars."

"Twenty thousand dollars is a lot of money to be laying around the house, in my opinion."

"My dad had two main interests; the first being guns. When he made trips to the old country he would invariably buy several nice Italian shotguns. Sometimes he would sell them when he got home. If he really liked one he'd keep it or trade it later. Most were quite expensive. Over the years the money from the sale of the guns added up."

"You said two interests."

"The other was playing poker. He was pretty good, too, from what I've heard. You've got to understand the real estate business in Monterey is a contact sport. He wasn't the only one with a lot of money. My father loved high stakes card games with the other big boys in town. The young bucks would really come after him. I heard a rumor he took some serious money off someone about a year ago. He didn't exactly want mom to know what was going on."

The twenty thousand dollars in the safe bothered McAllister. If robbery was the motive, the safe should have been empty.

"What about the staff?"

"Only two, a gardener and a housekeeper; a married couple. My parents liked to do most everything themselves, especially the cooking, which was mom's department. The staff is completely trustworthy. They've been with us for years."

"I have a piece of advice for you, Blue, based on a lot of experience in the murder business. Don't trust anybody for now."

When the detective force finished lunch they drove less than a mile to the police station. The chief was kind enough to see them. McAllister knew they were pushing the policeman a little but patience wasn't one of the detective's virtues. Palatine rose from his desk as they entered the office. McAllister tried to diffuse any confrontation between Palatine and Blue.

"Sorry to barge in on you chief. We know you're very busy. Blue was having lunch with us downtown so we thought we'd just stop by. Has anything come up yet?"

"As a matter of fact I was going to give you a call. I guess now is as good a time as any to fill you in. I drove up to Salinas to get an update on the truck yesterday. I don't think it's going to give us any good leads, other than the fact I believe your parents were killed at the ranch. It's obvious to me the area by the lake was the murder scene. I don't want to go into much detail but there's no way someone could have killed them somewhere else and then moved them up to the ranch and left them there. Let's take it as a given they were killed where you found them. No fingerprints were found on the truck. The fact the truck was in the water for five days probably destroyed any chance we might have had to find anything."

McAllister interrupted. "The shotgun in the back window bothers me a little. Was it loaded?"

47

"No. Investigators did find a box of shells in the glove box, though."

"So it looks like Enrico wasn't concerned about who he met."

"That's what's got us stumped. We're supposed to believe he drove all the way up to the ranch then way over to the big pond to meet with someone? He was at work all day so we're also supposed to believe he drove up there at night and didn't even load his gun? To me that would say he met someone he knew.

"This morning I got a call about another development. The blood in the kitchen at Blue's house is confusing, too. We'll know, eventually, who it belongs to when we get the DNA results back but in the meantime Salinas did a blood type analysis, which doesn't take long." The chief looked directly at Blue when he delivered the next piece of information. "Both of your parents were Type O, which is not entirely unexpected since that is the most common blood type. The blood in the kitchen was Type AB, the rarest blood type." A new piece of the puzzle had emerged. "Someone else got killed in the kitchen, or at least badly wounded."

Michael looked at Palatine. "Did you check all the hospitals in the county and see if a Type AB patient with a knife or gunshot wound checked in?"

"Being done as we speak. McAllister, what does the blood in the kitchen tell you?"

McAllister sat silent for a moment as he considered the new piece of information. "It must belong to one of the bad guys. If we get lucky and he has a record, the DNA will lead us right to the men responsible."

"County promised to do the best they could on the results. This is the biggest thing we've ever had come along here so you might as well know every agency wants to get in on it."

"You'll let us know as soon as you get the results?"

"Of course. The blood evidence is a big break in the case. In a couple of weeks we could have this thing wrapped up."

The chief stood, signaling the meeting was over. Outside Blue shared some new information with McAllister.

"Something's been bothering me. It's probably nothing but my father never put his shotgun in the rack behind the seat because he thought it made him look like a redneck. He always put it in a special case on the floor behind the seat. I remember seeing the shotgun in the garage on Wednesday, the day I drove up to San Jose. My dad had been cleaning it and left it on the bench at the back of the garage. I'm also pretty sure he would have taken a handgun with him if he was meeting someone."

"He owned hand guns, too?"

"He owned all kinds of guns."

"I'd like to have one more look at the house. Could we follow you over?"

Los Gatos was a small town, both in population and area. A few minutes later they arrived in tandem at the gate of a fine residence. Tanya's family had money but her mansion had nothing on the De Costa place. McAllister had visited Italy on two vacations. In the light of day the house looked like it had been flown over from the old country and gently placed in California.

"Blue, I have a question for you. Why do you still live at home?"

"Why do you ask?"

"Well, it just seems a little odd to me. You're about thirty years old, right?"

"Just turned twenty-nine. Italian boys usually stay home until they get married. My father has..." He almost choked. "My father kept me on a tight leash, so to speak. He paid me about fifty thousand dollars a year plus a company credit card for all my expenses. I didn't have access to an unlimited bank account by any means. I had to stay at home if I wanted to have money to buy my friends drinks when we went out."

"Okay, I guess that makes sense. It's obvious I don't know much about Italian family life. The most important thing now is did you notice anything out of place the night you came home? Think hard about it. Don't leave out the smallest detail."

"Follow me through the house. I'll have another look." They entered through the door at the side of the garage. "My room is down here by the kitchen."

The detective intervened. "The kitchen is upstairs."

"The extra kitchen."

"You have two kitchens?"

"You really don't know about Italians, do you? When family comes to visit from the old country we party for weeks. We have to keep two kitchens going to prepare all the food." The tour continued to the main level of the house, made up of a large living and dining room along with the main kitchen. Three more bedrooms made up another level, each with an en suite. "I only see one thing that seems out of place. It's pretty insignificant but my dad's Ferrari was not parked the way he normally left it."

"Show me what you mean."

They filed back down the stairs to the garage.

"You can see two parking spots on the right and one spot on the left. My mom drove the Buick Enclave and always parked in the spot closest to the kitchen. The old truck was always parked in the next spot. The last spot had its own door with a separate opener. Notice there's a little more room around the car on that side of the garage. Dad was a fanatic about his Ferrari. To him it was a status symbol, allowing him to show the world he was successful. He had his own spot in the underground garage at work, too. However, he would always back it into the garage. You can see it's pointed inward."

Tanya looked at Michael. "What could that mean?"

He looked each one in the eye before he answered. "I don't know yet but it's exactly the kind of thing I want you to tell me. Notice anything else?"

"I don't think so. The police had me go through the house with them, too, after the preliminary investigation. I didn't think about the Ferrari. Should I call them about it?"

"Keep it to yourself for now but keep thinking about the way the house looks. Let me know if you come up with anything else. You've been a big help, Blue. The gun was not right in the truck and there's something fishy about the Ferrari. I don't know what it means, yet, but I'll bet it's something."

Tanya and Michael said goodbye as they walked back to her Jag. On the drive home she wanted more information. "Michael, what do you make of the Ferrari and the shotgun?"

"A gun in the wrong place means someone else put it there. I'm sure the De Costas were taken from the house. The kidnappers must have noticed the gun on the work bench and put it in the truck to throw us off. A car parked in an unusual manner means someone else might have parked it or the old man was trying to leave a clue for Blue that something was wrong. They were kidnapped from the house all right. It had to have been at least three men. No, more than that. They had to drive at least two vehicles up to the ranch so they'd have a way to get back and also keep a gun on the De Costas. I'd say four. The blood in the kitchen will lead us to one of the four. He'll lead us to the others."

"Why didn't you say anything to Blue?"

"I don't want to influence what he tells me. I want him to keep thinking about the house in case he remembers something else out of place. I was also testing him."

"Testing him? What do you mean?"

"I'm still not one hundred per cent sure he isn't involved. I wanted to see if he gave me the same answers he gave Palatine. The chief already told me everything I asked Blue about today. I was checking to see if he would give me the same story. It's easy to slip up if you're lying."

"You think Blue might have killed his own parents?"

"An immediate family member is always a suspect. After all, he had a lot to gain. I'm not ruling him out, at least not from what I know so far. The blood could belong to someone who helped him murder his parents."

"You don't trust anybody, do you?"

"I trust you, princess, but trusting the wrong person can get you killed in this business."

Chapter 9

No detective business occurred the following day because it was time for Tanya to spring a surprise on her uncle, Peter Stafford. A dinner was arranged at Peter's house in San Francisco; an intimate affair with just Peter, Tanya and Michael being joined by Tanya's mother. Peter's physical transformation was amazing to Michael considering he'd been a drug addict for many years. Rigorous walks down to the marina, and most importantly, back up to the house, had paid dividends. Clear eyes and rosier skin attested to a much healthier looking man than when McAllister had first met him. Possibly he'd even gained a little weight. A strong gust of wind might not blow him around anymore.

Maria had stocked groceries per Tanya's instructions but it was family only for the night. During dinner Michael was blind-sided by a minor assault from Tanya's mother.

"Michael, is it true you're working on a case in Los Gatos?"

"Against my better judgment I agreed to get involved in the investigation of a double murder. I'm not on anyone's payroll, just having a look. It should be over soon."

"It seems an unnecessary danger to me."

Tanya flushed. "Mother, please. Could we talk about this later?"

"Your mother is right, Tanya. Any case can be dangerous. The smart move would have been to walk away."

"I hold you accountable for the safety of my daughter. If anything were ever to happen to her, I don't think I could ever forgive you."

The comment put a damper on dinner for a few minutes. After they finished dessert it was time for the surprise. Tanya could hardly wait to unveil the trick she had played.

"Peter, I want to show you something in the basement."

"You want to show me something in my own basement?"

His interest piqued, they walked together to the garage and rode the turn-table down a level. Tanya had told Michael previously she'd used Maria to alert her as to when Peter would be gone for a few hours. The basement was well lit as they viewed a row of classic Jaguars; the Mark IV saloon first, the alloy XK120, and then the surprise, the D-type! Peter seemed shocked.

"How did you get the D-type back?"

"You pulled a fast one on me when you decided to auction it at Pebble Beach last year. I texted one of the agents I knew at the auction so she could perform a phone bid to win the car. Mom acted as the bank. I guess she didn't mind investing in your rehab center. We've hidden it in the garage at her townhouse for the past year even though you've been over for dinner a couple of times. We had a few close calls making sure you didn't wander out to the garage."

Peter walked over and ran his hand along the lines of the car. "I love this car. I didn't want to give it up but I thought I had to make some kind of sacrifice for the treatment center. Writing a check was too easy."

"Well, we've managed to keep it in the family after all and I don't think we're going to let it get away again."

After dinner Tanya and her mom excused themselves to the kitchen. Peter and Michael enjoyed an unseasonably warm evening by the Koi pond. Michael declined the offer of a fine cigar but Peter seemed to enjoy the one he selected.

"Tell me about this case you're on. Tanya's hardly mentioned it to me."

"An Italian family owned extensive olive groves in what became Silicon Valley. The family sold the land, relocated to Monterey and invested the enormous profits in local real estate. The mother and father went missing recently and their son came to us for help. I suggested a search by helicopter which resulted in the discovery of the bodies in a small lake on a ranch they own up in the mountains. I'm sure they were kidnapped from their home. The case is confusing because I can't figure out a motive. The police found money in the safe at the house so it doesn't look like a robbery. Now the son wants me to find out who murdered his parents but it's not out the question he's behind the whole thing. I should have said no when he asked for help but Tanya couldn't resist. It's impossible for her to say no to someone in need."

"It sounds like you've been hired."

"The son, his name is Valentino De Costa by the way, tried but I wouldn't bite. Like I said, he might be in on it. My instincts say no but he's certainly inherited a lot of money. I want to be able to get out of the investigation as soon as I can."

"You seem particularly troubled by this case. What's bothering you?"

Michael paused as he tried to figure out the best way to answer Peter's question.

"Peter, you know a thing or two about addictions. I think you can see a little bit of the same thing in me with these cases. Once I get started I can't stop. I don't think it's a particularly good use of my time to get involved with a bunch of crooks and murderers. I think Tanya's mother was right on target about putting her in a dangerous situation. I should've stayed out of it. It would've been better if I had but Tanya couldn't refuse when De Costa asked for help. She's in denial about how these cases could affect us. I'd consider it a huge favor if you'd try to say something to her the next time you have lunch or coffee."

Peter agreed to try to help with Tanya but Michael knew it was already too late for the De Costa matter. Nothing would deflect the detective's interest from the case until it was solved. Solving murder cases was 24/7, not the kind of pastime for rich people.

Michael and Tanya decided to spend the night at Peter's house rather than make the drive home late in the evening. She came up with a good plan to keep him in bed till mid-morning. By the time they hit the road for the trip back to Los Gatos the rush hour traffic had subsided. In the afternoon Tanya made a valiant attempt to get back to work. Michael decided any business he could dream up could wait another day. Just when he thought the day was fully wasted his cell phone rang. Surprisingly, Tanya's mother's name was featured on the display. Odd, he thought, because she never called him, always Tanya. She blurted out the news.

"It's Peter. He's dead." Michael couldn't process the information for a moment. He managed to mumble a question about what had happened. "He died of a heart attack this afternoon. I got a call from the hospital. You've got to tell Tanya. Is she there with you now?"

"Yes, she's with me. I can't believe it. He looked so good yesterday. I'll talk to Tanya in a minute. I'll have her call you back when she can."

Tanya was chatting away on her cell phone with Gio, her contractor and partner in the renovation business; coffee cup in hand as she leaned on the kitchen counter. Michael tried to wait until she finished but Tanya seemed to sense from Michael's expression something was wrong and quickly finished the conversation. Michael held her close and tried valiantly to say something wonderful but all he got out was, "Peter." Tanya's legs almost gave way when she heard the name. After a few minutes she was able to call her mother, and then they immediately retraced their trip to the Stafford house so Tanya and her mother could make the arrangements for a funeral.

Breakfast was a grim affair the next morning when Tanya's cell phone rang. She mumbled affirmatively into her cell phone and quickly ended the call. She spoke directly to her mother. "Mr. Grover needs to meet with us as soon as possible. I told him he could come by at eleven. Something to do with Peter's will." Tanya explained to Michael that Grover was the family attorney.

The doorbell signaled Grover was punctual. Tanya assembled all, including Michael, in the formal den on the first floor, a room seldom used in the house and filled with books giving it a bit of a look of a lawyer's office. McAllister eyed the man carefully. The luster of his razor fine pin-striped suit fabric shouted expensive, as did the shine on his black oxfords. His thick, wavy silver hair finished off a carefully orchestrated look. McAllister decided being a lawyer to rich people was a tricky business but if you could pull it off, life could be very good.

"Tanya, I'm very sorry to trouble you at a time like this but there's business you must attend to immediately. I need to inform you of the contents of Peter's will."

"Let's get it over with as quickly as possible."

"I doubt many people, other than your mother, fully understood what a genius Peter was in the business world. He didn't just start an extremely successful company. When he cashed out in the eighties, he bank-rolled a lot of the technical start-up companies because he'd trained those same youngsters at his company. Showing little favoritism, Peter invested with just about everyone who had ever worked for him. Some of them went bust but a few did well." He paused a moment for effect. "Very well, in fact. His cash value, not including the house, was in excess of a billion dollars." Tanya audibly gasped but the attorney didn't miss a beat. "Well over a billion, actually. Maybe now you can see why my visit couldn't wait. His will essentially split the estate two ways; about three quarters to you and the rest to his rehab center. He took very good care of Maria and of course a few other incidentals had to be dealt with but basically that's how it works out.

"The house has been left to you as well; all the material things, actually. You're going to have to decide what to do with it. There is also the issue of who will take over management of the rehab center project. Peter expressed a desire that your mother take a place on the board of directors of the facility but hopefully someday you might want to step in." Another pause. "One final item affects Mr. McAllister." He turned his gaze to Michael, unable to disguise a look of envy. "Peter left you ten million dollars. I need to know how to transfer the money."

Michael thought he must have heard something wrong. He looked to Tanya for an explanation.

She smiled gently, not her wicked version. "I guess that's the going rate for saving the life of a billionaire's favorite niece."

"Would you have a blank check with you, Mister McAllister? We could transfer the funds automatically."

"No. I don't make a habit of carrying my checkbook with me. I'm not sure what to do."

Tanya came to the rescue. "I'll handle it with my phone when we get home."

The koi pond beckoned to Michael along with an ice cold Diet Dr. Pepper while Tanya signed documents. Her face was ashen when she joined him a few minutes later. He stood, hugged her tightly and whispered in her ear.

"We're going to have to install some serious security around the place in Los Gatos."

"Here, too. I'm not selling this house. It's like home to me. You know what my mother told me when Grover left?"

"No idea."

"Peter's been investing her money, too, ever since my dad died."

A strange sense of foreboding enshrouded Michael. His father had left him some money but he didn't breathe the same air as Tanya and her mother, even counting the magnanimous gift from Peter. Body guards and ultra-high security seemed likely, maybe even name badges like a corporate office. He wasn't too sure about an Oklahoma cowboy fitting in very well.

Chapter 10

McAllister's cell phone rang at just the instant he parked Tanya's Jag in the garage in Los Gatos a few days later. The display showed De Costa.

"I thought you might be interested to know the police made an arrest in my parents' case." Michael welcomed anything that didn't remind him of Peter and the funeral.

"Good. Who was it?"

"Three drug dealers from Watsonville."

"Drug dealers? Are the police trying to connect them to your parents?"

"I have no idea."

"How did you find out about the arrest?"

"A Monterey detective name Monroe called me late last night. He said he solved the case, making the arrests himself. I wanted to ask questions but he cut me off. He practically hung up on me. I tried to call Palatine but I couldn't reach him."

"I didn't think the Monterey Police were involved with the case. Let me go down to the station by myself. I'll corner the chief one way or another and find out what's going on. I'll call you as soon as I finish talking to him."

McAllister's visit didn't seem to surprise the chief. The meeting began with a brief staring contest.

"Can you fill me in on the arrests?"

"I heard about it late last night so this morning I called down to Monterey to find out what happened. The front desk seemed to be expecting my call because I was immediately transferred to a detective named Monroe, who turned out to be a real asshole.

"He talked down to me like he was a big-shot; threw me a few scraps about the investigation. Seems he found out about a fresh meth lab site up on the ranch. Said he had the case all wrapped up. Basically, he told me to mind my own business."

"A meth lab? Are you telling me the De Costas were involved in the drug business?"

"No. It's more likely some drug dealers used the property to cook up a batch of meth because of the remote location. Monroe thought Enrico suspected something was going on at the ranch and drove up to investigate. Apparently he got himself killed for it."

They both sat in silence again for a moment. As much as he wanted the case over, McAllister needed to make sense of the murders.

"How did Monroe and the Monterey police get involved?"

"His excuse was he had a snitch. When he got the names he made the arrests so he could grill them. Apparently he started on his suspects well before he brought them to the station. Each one tried to pin the murders on one of the others. Three of them from Watsonville. Just kids; hardly more than teen-agers. He said they all eventually confessed."

"What would possibly cause Enrico to drive all the way up to the ranch at night to check out a report of drug dealers? It seems to me he'd take some back up."

"You and I think the same way. Monroe didn't want to go into details. He just acted like he's some kind of miracle detective."

"Where is Watsonville?"

"It's down near Monterey but inland a few miles. Not a real big community. Lots of Latinos. Strawberry country.

The chief seemed to let his frustrations with the case get the better of him. "It seems to me like every piece of evidence we get on this case makes the whole thing more confusing." He paused and gave McAllister a cool, hard stare. "I'm going to trust you with something. You need to promise me to keep it between us." McAllister gave him a nod. "Something else bothered me when I went up to Salinas. The victim's clothes were laid out in plastic bags on a big table. On one end old man De Costa's clothes looked like he'd come straight from the office; Armani suit, fancy leather shoes. Not the kind of thing I would wear to chase down some drug dealers in the middle of the night up at the ranch. On the other end of the table his wife's clothes were arranged the same way. Hers, however, were quite casual; jeans and a sweater, but she was wearing house slippers. Now if De Costa takes his wife along with him to shoot it out with drug dealers, I don't think she'd wear her house slippers."

A little throbbing at the back of his head told McAllister he had to trust Chief Palatine.

"I spent some time with Blue after we left the other day. He noticed two things that seemed out of place. The first was the rifle in the gun rack inside the cab of the pick-up."

"What's strange about that?"

"Blue said his father never carried his shotgun that way because he thought it made him look like a red neck. Enrico always carried the rifle in a special case on the floor behind the seat when he drove the truck. Blue said the rifle was on the work bench in the garage the last time he saw it. Whoever pulled off the murders put the gun in the truck but didn't know it should have been in a case behind the seat. I'd bet money the case is still on the work bench in the garage."

"What else?"

"The Ferrari was parked nose in. Blue said his father always backed it into the garage when he came home."

"So if you were a detective working for me, what would these two facts mean to you?"

"I would say De Costa was under someone's control when he came home from work."

"Go on."

"I'm sure he was trying to leave a sign for Blue. Whoever was controlling him wouldn't know he usually parked the car the opposite way, but I think he was trying to show something was wrong."

"If he was in trouble, really big trouble, why would he go home and get his wife? Why would he put her in danger?"

"Maybe they had a gun on him."

"I don't think De Costa could be forced to take someone to his house and put his wife in danger even at gunpoint."

The chief made a good point. McAllister mulled it over for a second.

"Maybe they had a gun on her. Maybe they called him at work and told him to come home; no monkey business or his wife gets it. The slippers back that up, too. She was trying to leave a sign as well that something was wrong. Blue mentioned they always left their shoes at the door and slipped on house shoes when they came home. I saw his at the door, fancy leather ones. I don't remember the brand."

The chief paused again, even longer this time. "When were you going to share the information Blue gave you?"

Michael tried to mask a look of guilt he was sure was painted on his face. "Did you hear about Tanya's uncle?"

"We watch the news in Los Gatos."

"It kind of threw our house into a spin for a while. This is the first chance I've had to talk to you about it."

McAllister was on the receiving end of another long, cold stare from the chief before he continued. "I need to be able to trust you. If I don't feel I can, I won't share any more information with you."

"It won't happen again. If I find out something I'll let you know immediately."

"This case could get dangerous for you and Tanya. Whoever did this might go after Blue or it still might even be Blue in the middle of it. Maybe Blue's using you to get information from me. You'd better be very careful. I suggest you fill out a gun permit with me and start carrying. It's one thing to get yourself killed. It's quite another to have something really bad happen to your girl."

Tanya's mother's comments reverberated in Michael's ears. "You've got a point. Why don't I fill out the paperwork for an investigator's license and a gun permit before I leave?"

"I think that would be a very good idea. I'm going down to Monterey and nose around. I've still got some connections there."

The forms delayed McAllister an additional thirty minutes. The detective didn't like the idea of carrying a gun but he also felt the chief had given him some good advice. Tanya's protection was job one, especially in light of the mega fortune she'd just inherited.

Chapter 11

A black and white SUV with a silver star emblazoned on the side hustled west to Santa Cruz and then south along the coast. Traffic on the Pacific Coast Highway spoiled a splendid view of the ocean. By the time he arrived at the Monterey Police station an hour later Palatine was steaming. His secret parking spot behind the building waited for him obediently. Upon arriving at the front desk, the first words out of his mouth requested a face to face with a detective named Monroe. When Monroe showed up a few minutes later, he wore a sheepish grin.

"Chief, I can't believe you drove all the way down here. Why didn't you call first? I could've told you whatever you needed to know over the phone and saved you the trip."

Beady eyes darting below thinning, greasy hair gave him a weasel-like appearance and a pointed nose and pock-marked skin finished the picture. He had a tough presence about him, though, like he had experience knocking guys around; guys who thought right up to the minute they got the shit beat out of them they were bigger and tougher. Palatine didn't have to worry about such mundane things. No one was tough enough to give him trouble of a physical nature.

"I want to see the sheets on the suspects."

"Sure, but they're not suspects. They've already confessed."

After a few minutes Monroe produced a pile of papers. The chief quickly confirmed the suspects were indeed Latino boys, all three late teen or early twenties. One of the names caught his eye, possibly the younger brother of a man he'd arrested a few years back.

"I want to talk to Sanchez."

"Why? Like I said, they've already confessed."

"Do I need to talk to your chief?"

Monroe's face instantly turned red.

"No, that won't be necessary. We'll grant you every privilege. Give me a few minutes so I can put him in a room."

Twenty minutes later Monroe led Chief Palatine to the interview room. When Monroe decided to join the party, Palatine held out a tree-like arm.

"I'd like to handle this one by myself if you don't mind."

"Kid could be dangerous. He's already killed two people, chief."

"I'll take my chances."

The detective was left with a quizzed look on his face as the chief closed the door behind him. Inside he found a young, obviously scared, teen wringing his hands at the table. Both eyes were deeply bruised, one almost completely swollen shut. His bottom lip was also cut; the slit showing in an angry red. The suspect wore a small muscle type t-shirt and jeans, revealing dark skin free of tattoos. At least it seemed he wasn't linked to a gang. When the chief took the chair across from the accused, he leaned close and whispered.

"You remember when I arrested your brother?"

"Yes."

"Talk quietly so they can't record what we're saying. Did you kill the De Costas?"

"No, sir."

"They say you confessed."

"A cop beat the shit out of me. I thought he was going to kill all three of us. I would have said anything to get him to bring us to the station."

"Were you cooking meth up at the ranch?"

The young man dropped his head and nodded.

"Did De Costa catch you?"

"No one could've found us there in a million years."

"Did you see anybody at the ranch?"

"No."

"Your brother always carried a chrome-plated forty-five if I remember correctly. I assume since he's in prison you're carrying it now."

"Yes."

"Did you know the De Costas were killed with a forty-five?" The suspect's head dropped lower, the body language of a man realizing for the first time he'd been set up. "Are you telling me you didn't shoot them with your forty-five, even if the police come up with a match to your gun?"

"No."

"Okay. You know I'm an honest cop, right? I arrested your brother and put him away but I didn't plant any evidence on him or anything like that. He was guilty as hell." Again, a nod. "Keep your mouth shut from now on. I'm going to try to help you. Do you have an attorney?"

"No."

"Tell the next person you see you want an attorney. The authorities will have to appoint one for you. Don't talk to the police anymore without an attorney present. I'm going to try and get you out of the murder charges. You're on your own with the drug stuff."

The boy looked confused as the chief left but Palatine had what he wanted. When he left the interrogation room Monroe was still outside.

"I'll walk out with you, chief."

Monroe headed down the hall towards the parking lot at a brisk pace. Palatine let him get most of the way down the hall and then turned in the other direction toward the Monterey chief's office. Arriving at the door before Monroe could catch up; he opened with an insult, chief to chief.

"Why aren't you out catching bad guys?"

"Sean, get your ass in here. Can I get you a coffee?"

Palatine turned to look back down the hall as he entered the office. Monroe tried valiantly to catch up and sit in on the meeting but Palatine shut the door in his face.

"Dave, I need to talk to you seriously, off the record."

Dave Speer was a silver haired old school cop; commanding the Monterey force for almost fifteen years. Lean, despite his age, he still looked like a marine capable of leading an invasion. After serving in Special Forces in Viet Nam he'd joined the police force in Monterey and then worked his way to the top over the last thirty years. Sean looked up to him as the prototypical police chief. Palatine's first job was on the beat under him in Monterey. The Speer mantra was everything by the book. Speer's spotless record did the trick when Palatine pursued the head job in Los Gatos.

"I want to talk to you about those Latinos boys Monroe thinks are murderers."

Chief Speer gave him a long, serious look. "I can tell you already have an opinion on the matter."

"Those babies you've got locked up downstairs had nothing to do with the De Costa case."

"This is off the record, right?" Palatine nodded. "I took a fishing trip offshore for two days. I'd been putting in a lot of hours lately so Mary pushed me into it. She said I needed a little rest. I got back last night and today I find out Monroe beat the crap out of some suspects to get a confession. The DA's been on my ass all morning. I'm positive those boys are going to walk. We won't even be able to charge them on the drug rap."

"Why would he do such a stupid thing?"

"I don't know but I have to be careful if I try to fire him. The whole mess will get politicized to the point I'll have to jump through all kinds of hoops. The process could take months. In the meantime the shit is really going to hit the fan. My job might even be on the line if I can't keep this situation under control."

"Where did Monroe come from, anyway? He wasn't here when I was serving in Monterey and yet he's a detective."

"He came from Los Angeles with some good recommendations. Now I think they just wanted to get rid of him."

"Well, let me know if anything else develops." Sean rose, shook hands with his counterpart and left. Palatine noticed Monroe had pulled a disappearing act as he walked down the hall to his truck.

Chapter 12

The over-sized leather chair behind his father's desk still didn't feel comfortable. Blue only hoped he would be able to grow into it over time. The staff immediately acknowledged he was the new boss but the job weighed uncomfortably on his shoulders. He remembered how amused the staff had been when he first started accompanying his father to work; a recent graduate of San Jose State University. Eight years later he was forced to assume control. Fifty-odd men and women on the payroll, as well as their families, depended on him to make good decisions. Time would tell if a lifetime of training had been well spent. Even with self-doubt camped on his shoulder, he had to project confidence and leadership at every moment. The buzz of the intercom jolted him out of his daydream.

"Mister De Costa, a mister Patrick Reed is here to see you."

Blue had observed Patrick Reed make proposals to his father several times previously. His father intimated he didn't think much of the presentations.

"Send him in."

Blue stood, shook hands and motioned to the seat across from the desk when Reed entered.

"I was very sorry to hear about your parents. If there is anything I can do for you, please let me know."

"Thank you very much." Blue eyed Reed suspiciously; trying to figure out the reason for the visit. A direct approach seemed appropriate. "What is your business?"

"Your father signed a contract with me recently. I wanted to discuss it with you."

"I don't know anything about a contract. Do you have a copy with you?"

Reed opened a small leather attaché case and slid several papers over to Blue. With a quick scan Blue could tell it was the same deal that had been offered previously. However, the agreement appeared to bear the authentic signature of Enrico De Costa.

"My father sold you a group of buildings downtown for development including financing?"

"Yes. As you know we've been negotiating for some time about these properties. I guess Enrico finally decided to give me a break."

"Strange he didn't mention it to me."

"I don't know how you and your father run the business but I'm surprised you don't know about this agreement." Blue decided to keep quiet and see if Reed could come up with a plausible explanation. "I'll make you an offer since this comes as a surprise. This is an original contract. Why don't you keep it so you can consider the proposal? If you don't feel comfortable with the deal, tear it up."

The offer surprised Blue.

"I'd appreciate that. I'll study the agreement and get back to you. In the meantime I'll keep the contract here in my safe."

Reed seemed to hesitate for a moment, as if he wanted to say something else, but thought better of it.

"Very well, then. I'll wait to hear from you."

Blue noticed Reed's hand was sweaty when they shook at the end of the brief meeting; exiting the office like a rattlesnake was trying to climb up his pant leg. The apparent legitimate contract didn't make sense to Blue. His father had counseled him on the proposal several times, always advising against selling the property to an outsider. What would change his mind? What could Reed's angle be by allowing him to keep the contract and back out of the deal? A careful scrutiny of the signature seemed to clarify its legitimacy. The bold strokes would have been almost impossible to forge. A quick check of the files in the desk showed nothing about a new deal coming in. When Blue opened the wall safe he was shocked to find a second original of the agreement. Only he or his father would have been able to put the contract in the safe. Blue returned all the documents to the safe and gave the dial a spin. The heir to the De Costa fortune decided McAllister might be able to offer some advice.

"Michael, a strange thing just happened."

Blue quickly related the details of the meeting and the information about the second contract in the safe.

The detective knew the right question to ask. "What was the date on the contract?"

Blue had been too busy studying the details of the agreement to check the date, which turned out to be the very day his parents disappeared.

"This might be the break we've been hoping for. What time did you leave for San Jose that day?"

"I'd say between two and three."

"You were with him all day until you left?"

"Yes. I followed him to the office in my truck because I knew I was leaving early but we even had lunch together before I left."

"Check with your receptionist. See if she remembers a meeting late in the day. The chief didn't find any appointments on the schedule but that doesn't rule out something spur of the moment. If she doesn't know anything, find out when she left."

"He doesn't seem the type."

"Who doesn't seem the type?"

"Reed. The guy with the contract. He doesn't seem the type to be mixed up in this. I don't see him getting the best of my dad."

"He just admitted to being one of the last people to see your father alive, even if he didn't realize it. Admitting this meeting to you was a very stupid thing to do, in my opinion. Reed's going to the top of my list. We need to talk about this. Do you have time to come over to our place this evening?"

"I'll make time."

"Make it seven. I'll leave the gate open."

Chapter 13

McAllister loafed in the hot tub during the early afternoon, rolling things around in his head and playing what-if games. The age old challenge was to make sense of the facts on hand. The meaning was always there for the taking. Later he found his new Gibson guitar and plugged it into an ancient Fender amp. While continuing to play the possibilities through his mind, he tried his best Clapton imitation. The sound-proofing Tanya had built into the room downstairs seemed well conceived.

Tanya, Valentino and Michael circled the kitchen counter just after seven, a cappuccino in front of Blue and Tanya. Tanya slid Michael an ice cold can of Diet Dr. Pepper from the refrigerator just before the meeting started. Blue didn't waste time.

"I guess you can tell the chief doesn't like to be seen talking with me. He thinks it makes him look bad, like I have undue influence on him. Palatine doesn't seem to mind working with you, though. I guess you police officers stick together. I was hoping you could at least keep me up to date with what's going on with the case."

"Let's start with the facts and go from there."

"What about the three kids arrested?"

"I don't know much about them yet. The chief was going to look into it today so maybe he'll have something soon." Michael threw a glance at Tanya, who looked like it was taking every ounce of control she had to keep from interrupting. "In my opinion, though, the big break in the case came today when you met with this Patrick Reed character. I'd like you to tell me about the meeting in detail, if you don't mind."

"Reed came to the office without an appointment, wanting to discuss an agreement."

McAllister quickly interrupted. "What about his mannerisms? Did he seem nervous?"

"Yes. I noticed he was quite nervous the whole time he was in my office."

"Okay. Good. Go on."

"My father had carefully analyzed the deal, which had been suggested several times over the past year or so, but he indicated we would never go through with it. The idea for the development wasn't bad but the land was too valuable to let it go to someone outside the family. What I found very strange was Reed left the contract with me. He said if I wasn't comfortable with the deal I could tear it up. Now if he tried to force the deal on me I would say Reed's involved somehow. But he gave me the contract and told me I could do what I wanted."

"Did the receptionist remember a meeting with Reed?"

"No, she said the office was pretty quiet after I left. My dad just worked on the phone."

"What time did she leave the office?"

"She said my father let her take off around four so she could miss traffic going home."

Michael took a sip of his Diet Dr. Pepper. The ice cold drink had a pleasant bite. He ran his hands through his hair before he spoke.

"Reed met with your father after four, setting your parent's abduction somewhere between four-thirty and six-thirty. Reed's placed himself right in the middle of the time line for the crime. Do you have one of his business cards?"

"Not with me but I do at the office."

"Call me when you get to work in the morning. I need to pay him a visit."

"Won't a meeting tip him off?"

"I guarantee you he'll never suspect a thing. Personally, I'm sure he's in on it. The blood on the kitchen floor couldn't have belonged to Reed, but it will probably be from an associate. If I can figure out two of the men involved, I've got a good chance of putting the whole thing together. I'll check with the chief tomorrow to see what he thinks. I could be wrong about the confessions but something tells me Reed is the key to finding out what happened. Now is what I call bulldog time."

Blue seemed confused. "What do you mean by that?"

"I'm going to chomp down on Mr. Reed's leg and not let go until I have this thing solved."

Blue rose from his chair and headed for the door but suddenly stopped and turned.

"Michael, could I talk to you for a minute by the car?"

Tanya quickly realized she wasn't invited. She seemed to decide it was important to strangle the coffee cups in the sink. The night air was cool when they stepped outside but McAllister didn't grab a jacket because he expected the conversation to be brief. Two bodyguards stood by Blue's truck as Michael was waved to an open area so the others couldn't hear what was to be discussed.

"I want to make something clear to you. I did some background on you before I came here the first time. You killed the Slasher with his own knife. Word is you killed a criminal in Tulsa, too; threw him out a window or something." McAllister didn't bother to correct him. Blue had something on his mind and the detective wanted him to get it out. "I don't want the police to catch whoever killed my parents."

"You don't want the killers to be caught?"

"I said I don't want the police to catch them. I want you to catch them and when you do, I want you to bring them to me." He paused a minute to let the statement soak in. "Am I making myself clear? I want you to bring them to me and a few of my closest friends. I don't want these murderers to spend a long time in prison leading an easy life. I want them to spend a very uncomfortable evening with me. Afterwards, well, I doubt if they'll ever be seen again. You could name your price for a scenario like that."

McAllister tried to calm himself before he responded. "I've been an officer of the court my whole working life. I go by the rules. You may think I'm an assassin but nothing could be further from the truth. I was trying to arrest both of the suspects you mentioned." He took a quick breath before he continued. "I'll try to find out who's responsible for your parents' deaths because it's the quickest way I can make the case go away. However, when I do, I'm finished with you. I know how you feel but when I find the bad guys, I'll give them to the cops. That's the only way I work. If that's not good enough for you, then quit calling me." McAllister turned to head inside then stopped. "Don't even think about going after Reed on your own. If you kill him I might not be able to figure out what happened. Give me some time and I promise you I'll get to the bottom of this."

Tanya used every trick she could think of that night, and she knew some good ones, but Michael wouldn't tell her what Blue offered. The detective knew only a fool would hope for justice. McAllister figured no matter what happened with the case, the end result wasn't going to feel like justice.

Chapter 14

McAllister's phone rang early the next morning. Blue gave him the details of Reed's office, which turned out to be in Santa Cruz; good news because it was a lot shorter drive than Monterey. The next step was a cell phone call to Palatine.

"I need to talk to you. We've got a new face in the De Costa killings. Looks like the break we've been waiting for."

"Lunch?"

"Works for me."

"Come to the station at noon. I know a place we can get a good sandwich and talk without being interrupted."

The chief drove. Crossing over the highway to Santa Cruz, he pulled in at a stand near a reservoir.

"Best barbeque in California." The good citizens of Los Gatos bought them each a sandwich and drink, which they carried across the access road. A small park with tables offered a pleasant view of the lake. McAllister realized the creek behind the Waldorf place emptied into what must be the city's water supply. The chief didn't waste time on formalities. "What have you got for me?"

"A guy named Patrick Reed visited Blue yesterday with a contract signed by the old man for a sweet deal on a real estate development in Monterey. The project had been discussed by the De Costas, father and son, several times. Enrico decided against it because the property offered too much upside to give to an outsider. Now two original contracts have shown up, one of them already in Blue's safe, with signatures that look legit. What surprised Blue was Reed gave him the other original contract. Reed said if De Costa didn't want to proceed he could tear up both agreements. The one in the safe could only have been put there by Enrico."

"What do you think it means?"

"One of two things. First, Reed has absolutely nothing to do with the murders. The fact he gave the contract to Blue backs up that theory."

"What's the other option?"

"Reed's in this up to his neck. The story gets better, too. The contracts were dated the day the De Costas disappeared. Blue left the office after lunch. The old man's receptionist left at four. Reed's admitted he was the last person to see Enrico alive, practically placing himself at the crime scene. I think the murders are related to the contract somehow but I haven't been able to figure that part out yet."

"If you were me, how would you proceed?"

"I'd have a good hard look at Reed. Eliminate him or get enough to put him away for the murders. The easiest way would be to go over his phone records."

"I'd have to get a judge in Santa Cruz involved. Their police would be right in the middle of it in no time. I think there's a better way."

Just before McAllister was going to find out about a better way, Palatine's phone rang. The chief put up a finger to call time out and walked a few paces away so he could talk privately. When he returned he shifted gears.

"Before we go any farther with Reed let me fill you in on what I found out yesterday. I drove down to Monterey to nose around. I think I told you I worked a beat there before I came here. I trained under the chief so I know my way around. Detective Monroe, the genius I was telling you about, was surprised to say the least when I showed up. He tried to keep me away from his murderers but I threatened to go to the top. Turned out I knew one of the suspects."

"How could you possibly know one of the suspects?"

"I put his older brother away. When I interviewed him he was scared shitless and beat to hell. Bottom line, he didn't confess to anything. The poor Latino kid thought Monroe was going to kill him and then frame him for the murders. He would've confessed to anything. I tricked him, though. It's a long story but I knew he owned a forty-five. I told him the De Costas were shot with a forty-five. He believed me so obviously he had no knowledge of the crime scene or any details about the murders. He couldn't have described the crime if his life depended on it.

"I met with the chief in Monterey before I left; a guy named Speer. Speer said Monroe's going to fry for beating up the suspects but it'll take some time to do it in a politically correct manner. The call I just took? Those Latino boys have been released. Their court appointed attorney got them sprung, pronto. Their lawyer will probably file charges for police brutality. All charges have been dropped against the suspects."

"Perfect. Now the suspects are untouchable. Monroe can say he found the right guys, but no one will be able to talk to them."

"Let's get back to Reed. Like I said, I think there's a better way of dealing with him. I'd prefer to have someone on the outside look into a few things. I don't want the Santa Cruz PD in on this yet and I also don't exactly want the sheriff nosing around either. Once they're in I lose any chance to work on the case on my own. It'll be a free for all. I have another good reason, too, but I don't want to go into a lot of details about why right now. I was thinking of a non-law enforcement investigation. I was thinking you fit the bill nicely. I'll find out what I can about Reed without raising any suspicion but you could take a little harder look, if you know what I mean. Don't get caught doing anything illegal. I stress the getting caught part more than the illegal. My ass will be on the line as much as yours."

McAllister nodded. Palatine retrieved some papers out of the console of his truck and dropped them in McAllister's lap on the way back to the station.

"You're officially registered as a private investigator in the state of California and your guns are registered. You should know what to do."

On the drive back to the house a million thoughts clouded McAllister's mind. The police chief's trust in him didn't sit well. Maybe two partners who had worked together for years would bend the law, but he'd just met Palatine. McAllister's previous career had taught him not to trust anyone. The investigation of Reed would have to be done very carefully and that meant he might not share everything he learned with anyone, not even the chief. One wrong move and the whole thing could back-fire on the detective. And more importantly, Tanya.

Chapter 15

Tanya made sure she was covered at work for the day since she'd officially designated herself as Michael's partner for the investigation of Patrick Reed. When she started planning the operation, McAllister thought of her mother's warning, but he knew it was too late to stop, rationalizing the situation by telling himself he could protect her best by keeping her with him.

Tanya broke his train of thought, "So where do we start?"

"Fire up your computer. Let's see what we can find out about Reed the easy way."

"My cell phone can handle that." McAllister was reminded of Tanya's smart phone mastery as her thumbs sped across the face in a blur, punishing the tiny device. After a quick sip of coffee she followed with round two, really putting the hurt on the digital keyboard in the process. It seemed Patrick Reed, LLC maintained a web site glamorizing a few projects in Santa Cruz but they seemed pretty small time to McAllister as his girl described them. The Monterey project would have been his entry into the big time.

"There's nothing much about his office, at least about his staff. I mapped the address of his office so we can find it without any trouble."

"Let's get cleaned up and have a look. One thing, though."

"What's that, boss?"

"You can't look fabulous while we're investigating. Try to find something to wear that's not the latest fashion, if that's possible with your wardrobe. No spiked heels. If anyone sees that tight ass of yours, they'll remember you. A ball cap and sunglasses would be a good idea."

"Well, I never thought about trying to look as bad as possible but I'll see what I can do."

Some pre-investigating in the shower caused a delay on their first day on the job. When Tanya came downstairs an hour later she was in disguise.

Modeling a pair of plain, non-designer jeans and a sweatshirt, she asked. "My cap and sunglasses are out in the car but otherwise, how do I look?"

"You're still the cutest girl I ever met."

Michael's opinion got him a smile and a kiss.

"I think it's impossible to hide my hotness. You'll have to provide a diversion of some kind."

He slapped her on her tight ass and pushed her towards the door. "Let's go."

She drove her car and headed to the coast. A modern Jaguar was not exactly the ideal non-descript car, but it was better than Lucille. His old Jag drew a crowd anywhere she went. Thirty minutes later they located Patrick Reed's office, a low rise building on Front Street. The area provided sidewalk performers, homeless people, the works; good cover while they investigated.

Tanya slowed as they passed their target then parked several blocks away. A perch on the sidewalk directly across the street from the building gave them a closer look.

"What now, Marlowe?"

"We're going to have to pay a visit to Reed's office. See what's up. When I say we, I mean you."

"I can't just walk into his office and ask to have a look around."

"You're going to pretend you're looking for a home in Santa Cruz. While you're inside look around as much as you can. Count the offices; estimate the size of the staff from what you can see from the lobby. Memorize everything. For example, how many children are with the woman standing by the door across the street? If you were carefully observing, you would have noticed."

"I didn't know I was supposed to be observing already. That's not fair."

"There isn't a woman across the street. I'll wait here at the cafe." He motioned over his shoulder. "I'll buy you a coffee if you do well."

She seemed excited as she crossed the street.

* * *

The elevator delivered Tanya to a door on the third floor that read Patrick Reed, LLC with a line below reading Real Estate in slightly smaller print. As she opened the door she found a sad reception area with a young woman at a desk. Tanya was surprised by the drab decor. Apparently making a good first impression was not part of Reed's business plan. She'd put some gum in her mouth during the elevator ride and exaggerated her chewing.

"Hi there, hon. I'm looking to buy a house in Santa Cruz and I'm loaded. Can someone help me, pronto? I'm kind of in a hurry."

The receptionist calmly appraised her.

"We're not realtors. We build commercial buildings. How did you hear about us?"

"I saw your name on the register downstairs. I've been shopping all morning."

"We build shopping malls; buildings like that. I think there's a realtor down a block to the west. You should try there."

Light shone from under a single office door off the reception area, indicating Patrick Reed was probably in.

"Gee, it's kind of a small office for a big real estate firm. How many employees do you have?"

"This is the owner's personal office, Mr. Patrick Reed. He contracts the work from here."

"I see. Well, thanks for the tip on the other office. I'll try them. Too bad you couldn't help me."

"Yes, it's our loss."

The receptionist shook her head as she returned to her paperwork.

* * *

Michael watched Tanya exit the building and jaywalk to his table.

"How'd you do?" He'd already paid for the coffee. Unfortunately Diet Dr. Pepper was not available so he had to deal with a substitute.

"You know, I think I'm pretty good at this detective business. Reed's layout consists of a single office with a receptionist outside to answer the phone and whatever. She said he contracts out the work on jobs."

"Do you think she suspected anything?"

"Absolutely not. Real estate was printed on the front door so I'm sure she bought it."

"Was Reed in?"

"The door to his office was closed but the light was on."

"Reed was probably there. The one-man office might make our job easier. We can just follow him and see where he goes."

McAllister thought about Blue's description of Reed; tall with bony features and bright red hair like steel wool. A suspect like that would have to set himself on fire to be any easier to track.

"Did the building have an underground parking lot?"

"You didn't ask me to check on parking."

"We'll have to find out what kind of car he drives so we can tail him next time. Enjoy your coffee for a minute. I'm going to take a quick look around."

The building didn't contain a parking garage but a back exit led to a large street level parking lot across an alley. Watching the front and back of the building would be impossible without help. McAllister was puzzling over the logistics as he walked back through the first floor lobby. The elevator door opened as he passed by and he almost ran into Reed, who excused himself on his way out the front.

Michael nodded to Tanya across the street as he followed him. Reed ducked into a restaurant a couple of blocks down. Tanya followed from the other side of the street. McAllister realized they had started so late it was already lunch time. The detective nodded back up the street to Tanya and was mildly amused as he watched her work her way back, totally incognito as she traversed the sidewalk. She peered into various store windows but never once in his direction.

On the way back to Los Gatos McAllister phoned Palatine. The chief invited the new detective team for a meeting. When they were shown into his office the chief stood and greeted them. He seemed stunned for a moment by Tanya, a common occurrence. She had that effect. McAllister thought it was mostly the blue eyes. After an introduction Palatine made a valiant effort to get down to business.

"How did you do on your first day?"

The detective got right to the point. "We ran up some big expenses. Reed's office in Santa Cruz is a one man affair with a receptionist to take calls. He contracts out his work so he doesn't need a lot of employees. We've got a couple of problems, though."

"I'm listening."

"We need to know what kind of car he drives and the license number. We also need to know where he lives. I think he has an unlisted phone number or he just uses his cell phone. We've got to figure out how to follow him when he leaves the office."

"Give me a few minutes and I'll get you what you need."

The chief walked outside and spoke in a soft tone with his admin. McAllister decided to push his luck when Palatine returned.

"Another thing. We need a piece of shit car. We both drive Jaguars, not the best for undercover work."

I have a perfect car out back. We recovered it in a stolen car ring. It's due to be auctioned next month. The car is just about invisible. I'll get you the keys."

McAllister followed Tanya back to the house. A simple formula existed for deciding if a car was a shit-mobile. This one fit so well it might have been the prototype. McAllister had Reed's home address and the details on his car. He figured in two days Reed would be the brother he never had.

Chapter 16

The next morning Tanya left early for a day on her project site. McAllister had some plans for her in the evening involving Reed. He decided it would be best to surprise her when she got home. A vague plan for the morning was interrupted by the jingle of his cell phone.

"McAllister."

"Stacy Carson from the Los Gatos PD. I need to talk to you."

"If this is about old cases, I really don't have the time now."

"This is important. I need to meet with you."

She sounded serious. McAllister was concerned about meeting her without talking to Palatine first but decided it was easier to ask for forgiveness later.

"Where do you want to meet?"

"I'll come pick you up. I don't want Palatine to see your old Jag around the station."

"Do you know where the old Waldorf place is located?"

"Yes. I'll be there in ten minutes."

When she arrived in five McAllister wondered if she'd called him on the way. She must have been pretty sure he'd cooperate.

"Would you like to come in for a coffee?"

"No time for that. I'm going to take you for a ride. You don't mind, do you?"

"What could possibly go wrong?" He sensed a little tension as they headed towards the coast. A little small talk seemed like a good way to break the ice. "How did you know where the Waldorf place was located?"

"We used to sneak in when we were teenagers. This was the number one make-out spot complete with a haunted house and a gravesite. I knew a secret way through the fence down by the creek."

"You grew up in Los Gatos?"

"Lived here my whole life."

"I heard your father was the chief before Palatine. He was killed in some kind of a traffic accident?"

"A drunk driver hit him head on not too far from here on the highway. My mom was with him."

McAllister instantly regretted the direction he'd taken with the small talk.

"Sorry. I shouldn't have brought it up."

"It's okay. It's been eight years. The police department carried a life insurance policy. I used the money to get my college degree in police science."

"I knew the same kind of officers in Tulsa where I grew up. The kids either followed their parents into the police business or ran as far away as possible."

"I love the job. I admired my father very much. He was good at his job. I always wanted to be a cop. Once I was in college, the science of the investigations kind of took hold of me."

She whipped her police cruiser south toward the coast until they hit Santa Cruz, and then took a hard left.

"Your girlfriend's a knock-out. I heard she's rich, too. How you'd manage that?"

"She's really cute but not very smart." McAllister decided it wasn't prudent to discuss his love life with a young, attractive woman. "Would you consider it impolite if I asked where we're going?"

"We're going to rattle those Latino boys a little and see what shakes out."

"The ones who were arrested in the De Costa murders?"

"The very ones. My dad had a history with them. The older one, the one Palatine arrested and put away; my dad was the one who was onto him. They're kind of like wannabe gang-bangers. I know where they hang out."

"This seems like an incredibly bad idea. I'm sure you must have a good reason."

"I do. Open the glove box."

Inside a Colt pistol lay wrapped in a shoulder holster.

"I want you to wear it under your jacket. I noticed you weren't carrying. If they look like they want trouble, let them see it."

McAllister decided the only upside at this point was he might be finished with any kind of investigations on a permanent basis.

"Why didn't you take Palatine along instead of me?"

"The chief told me to stay away. I think he might be hiding something. You'll understand when we get there. Just back me up."

Carson turned inland a few miles before Monterey. A sign on the edge of town announced Watsonville. In minutes they pulled up in front of an ancient one-story house with a few brave paint chips hanging on for dear life. Stacy banged on the screen door with a ferocity that left no doubt it would be a good idea to answer but no one took her advice. Taking a hard right she walked around to the back. The three banditos in question were sitting around a rusted metal table on what had once been a patio.

"Didn't you boys hear me knock at the front door?"

All three faces still showed scrapes and bruises from the beating by Monroe. The tallest one, McAllister estimated he hadn't been driving long, took charge.

"We don't like visits from cops. Our lawyer said you can't touch us. You're going to be in big trouble for coming here." He looked directly at McAllister. "Why don't you take off? Your little girlfriend can stay. We'll take good care of her for you."

Carson moved in a blur, drawing her gun in a fluid motion and pushing the big talker backwards in his chair. Before he could retaliate she straddled him on the ground with her gun pressed hard into his nose. The other two seemed like they wanted to get involved until Michael opened his jacket and gave them a good look at his gun.

"You're going to wish you were back in Monterey if you don't answer my questions." She jerked him off the ground, righted his chair and strongly suggested he start cooperating. McAllister helped her back the three of them against the house. "I want to know what's been going on around here before Monroe arrested you and beat you up. Tell me about your drug business."

Something about Stacy's charm changed the leader's heart. He decided to cooperate with all his might. "We've been selling some drugs. There's no other way to make a living around here for us. It's not the first time we've run into Monroe, though."

"I'm listening."

"He busted a few of our deals. Each time he took the drugs and the money."

"Just him or were there others?"

"Three of them. I think they're all cops because they flashed badges; laughing at us because they knew there was nothing we could do about it. The deal was we could keep selling but they were going to take a cut from time to time."

McAllister decided to join the fun. "Did one of them have red hair?"

"No. No red hair."

Stacy continued. "Did you see the city name on any of the badges?"

"It happened too fast. They looked real, though."

"I had a suspicion we were dealing with some dirty cops. I wanted to make sure. What you've said confirms it. My name is Officer Carson, Stacy Carson. If you want to file a report make sure you get my name right." McAllister thought they were done but she had one more item on her list. "I've got some news for you dumbasses." She seemed to like the chief's technical terms. "The police know who you are now. You're not going to be able to sell drugs around here, anymore. You need to find an honest way to earn a living. We've got good county training centers. Get enrolled in some classes and learn a trade. Otherwise, you're going to end up in prison just like your brothers. Your mothers want something better for you."

One of the suspects spat back at Carson. "Yeah, like we've got the money for a trade school. You're dreaming."

McAllister decided to barge in again. "Stacy, may I borrow your notebook?"

McAllister tore out a page and wrote his name and cell number.

"I'll pay for any trade school you want to attend. Here's my name and cell number. Call me any time." His offer seemed to shock the gang into silence. Stacy wanted to use the opportunity for a getaway but McAllister had one more question. "What were you guys doing all the way up at the De Costa ranch? That's a long way from here."

"Everybody knows about the ranch. It's a good place to mix up some meth. No one is going to disturb you. The place is hardly ever used."

When they were safely in the car heading back to Los Gatos Carson asked about McAllister's offer. "Did you really mean what you said back there about paying for school for those kids?"

"Absolutely. Education seems to cure just about every problem. I think they want a better life but don't know how to make it happen. I don't want to give them any excuses." They continued in silence for a minute. "You know if this gets back to the chief he's going to take a piece out of both of our asses."

"You better hang on tight, then, because we're going to see him right now."

A few minutes after arriving at the station Carson and McAllister found themselves sitting across from Palatine, updating him on the day's developments. When the chief got an inkling of what they'd been up to he slammed his office door and then turned back to face them.

"Stacy, I specifically told you to stay away from those guys. We're all going to end up in the shithouse."

"I told you we were dealing with dirty cops but you wouldn't listen to me. Now we know for sure. I want to know what you're going to do about it. What if Monroe's helpers are from Los Gatos?"

The scene reminded McAllister of a time he was in the principal's office in elementary school.

"I've been working on this, Stacy. I just didn't let you in on it. I didn't think you were involved in anything illegal but I can't trust anybody right now. That's why I've been using McAllister on the sly." The new piece of information seemed to surprise her. "Now you get back to your office and leave me and McAllister to our business." Carson expertly slammed the door when she left.

The chief turned his ire on McAllister. "This damn thing's completely out of control. What in the hell were you doing riding with her?"

McAllister tried with all his might to come up with something plausible to get himself off the hook but on such short notice he had nothing. Stacy saved him when she burst back into the room.

"Chief, we got a hit."

"Got a hit on what?"

"The blood evidence from the De Costa house belongs to an ex-con named Clarence Waters. He lives in Santa Cruz."

The chief snatched the fax out of her hands, almost ripping it apart as he read it.

"Stacy, you're grounded. Get back to your office and don't come out till quitting time."

She expertly re-slammed the door on her way out. The chief turned his attention to McAllister but before he could get nasty the detective tried to change the subject.

"This gun belongs to you. Stacy gave it to me while we were riding over to Watsonville." The chief carefully rolled the holster around the gun and deposited it in a lower drawer of his desk.

"You owe me one for this little stunt and I have an idea how to collect. Where are you parked?"

Chapter 17

The chief outlined a homework assignment while he drove McAllister home.

"The fax about Waters came from the county. I'm sure they're preparing a search warrant for his residence. Santa Cruz will plow right in, too. I'd like to get some inside information before they tear the place apart. You have any idea how I could do that?"

"You'll never beat them there if you try to go by the book."

"I agree. If I were to lay this fax down on the seat between us where you could kind of glance down at it, you might be able to read the address."

"True. And I might be able to go have a quick look at the house before anyone else got there."

"You'll be working on your own. If you get caught, I can't help you much."

"You wouldn't have a spare pair of rubber gloves, would you?"

"Try the glove box."

On the road south toward Santa Cruz Michael took the opportunity to call Tanya on his cell phone and fill her in on his schedule for the day. An off-handed comment she made rang a bell deep in his subconscious.

"You don't seem to have a problem breaking the law. I thought you were trained as a police officer?"

After a few seconds he spoke thoughts that had been bouncing around in his head for some time. "I followed the rules for twenty years. All it got me was kicked off the force and a child killed that I could have saved. I guess I've decided to take a few shortcuts, especially if I can catch some bad guys. They don't play by the rules. To catch them I have to level the playing field." It didn't sound any better saying the words out loud but he knew he had crossed over some kind of boundary.

A fifties looking bungalow raised on cinder blocks didn't look like it wanted to put up much of a fight as McAllister climbed the front steps to the porch, slipping on the pair of borrowed gloves as he walked. The mailbox hadn't seen much attention lately by the look of the envelopes crammed inside and balanced on top. The front screen was locked so McAllister worked his way around the side. The windows were beyond reach so he continued to the back door, which he found locked as well. The porch offered good access to a window, though. McAllister worked his pocket knife through a small gap and turned the lock. After sliding the lower pane up, he stepped inside.

Job one was the mailbox so he immediately returned to the front of the house, unlocked both door and screen and recovered the mail, bringing it inside and depositing the contents in a heap on a battered kitchen table. Most of it was junk but a water bill showed a post mark about the time the elder De Costa disappeared, a fact McAllister decided didn't bode well for Clarence's survival. A layer of dust on the table agreed with that scenario.

A checkbook discovered inside the bedroom dresser showed a balance of just under a thousand dollars. Something inside a cowboy boot in the closet proved more interesting. A fat roll of bills was just visible to an eye that had learned to look for such things. The detective withdrew the roll by placing his pocket knife in the center and giving the boot a gentle shake upside down. After spreading the notes on the table near the mail he counted over eight thousand dollars; a pretty good stash for a con out of prison only a few months. Rerolling the bills he carefully returned them to the boot. Few clothes graced the closet and the furnishings of the house matched the wardrobe. After returning the mail, sans a few pieces of junk which he left on the table, he left via the back window, leaving it unlocked this time.

On the way home he thought of Stacy's words: "What if we have some dirty cops in Los Gatos?" What if one of them was the chief? It suddenly occurred to McAllister how easy it would have been for the chief to make a phone call to the police in Santa Cruz and trap him in Waters' house, possibly incriminating the detective with the other suspects. Michael quietly repeated his recent advice to Blue. "Don't trust anybody."

Chapter 18

Michael was starving by the time Tanya arrived home for dinner but she was wondering about something of a completely different nature.

"Have you planned something romantic for this evening? After all, it's Friday night."

"I've come up with a completely unique experience for you. We're going to stake out Reed's house; see if he goes out."

The glamour of the detective business seemed to be fading quickly as far as Tanya was concerned.

"How late could it be?"

"If he goes out I'll follow him wherever he goes. If he stays in We'll leave when the lights go out. Those are the rules in the handbook for detectives regarding stake-outs."

"I'll go with you tonight but I'm not sure about afterwards."

The shit-mobile rolled up near Reed's place around nine. McAllister had learned a rule from years as a detective: Darkness made bad men feel safe. Around eleven Reed's Lexus shot out of the alley and accelerated away from them. The action seemed to excite Tanya.

"What if we lose him? Can he see us?"

"The shit-mobile is invisible. If we lose him we'll have to cruise through town until we find his car. Otherwise we have to start all over tomorrow night."

Her voice increased noticeably in intensity. "You're letting him get too far ahead. Close it up!"

A bright red sports car didn't prove much of a challenge to follow. The bustling wharf appeared in minutes. Tanya leapt from the car and kept an eye on Reed while Michael found a parking spot on the street. Their flame-topped target headed to a bar called the Red Parrot. A youthful crowd seemed to be looking for excitement, which made for a high energy vibe. The noise level made a strategy session impossible. Reed seemed to know where he was going; quickly taking a spot at a long wooden bar over-looking the sea. Spotlights mounted on the roof shone out to the ocean providing a stage for the waves to perform. Cool air invaded the establishment through large open windows, reeking of fish or seagulls or possibly rotten wood, McAllister wasn't sure which. Soon Reed was joined by another man. Michael and Tanya took a place at the same rail but at a safe distance making a good look at the second man difficult. Holding their faces close together, the two men spoke as if they wanted to make sure no one could overhear what they were saying. Their discussion seemed heated; possibly an argument. An envelope passed from the stranger to Reed.

McAllister spoke close to Tanya's ear. "We need to know the identity of the other man. We'll follow him when he leaves. Reed will probably head home."

After twenty minutes Reed and his companion paid their bill and left. McAllister left a twenty under his glass so they could make a quick get-away.

"Tanya, follow the other guy and find out what kind of car he's driving. I'll get our car and pick you up. Call me on your cell phone and keep talking to me while you follow him. I need to know if you get into trouble."

McAllister sprinted down the street to retrieve the car while balancing his cell phone to his ear and returned just in time to pick up Tanya without losing their target. The stranger headed south on the Pacific Coast Highway in a non-descript sedan, not as invisible as the shit-mobile, but a close cousin. McAllister stayed as far back as possible without losing him, a little too far to get the plate number. When they arrived in downtown Monterey thirty minutes later their quarry just made a light the detective team missed. McAllister waited a second and clicked his bright lights on the steering column, causing the light to turn back to green.

"How did you do that?"

"It depends on the city but many times after ten the lights on smaller streets will change if you hit your bright lights."

McAllister hustled to an intersection ahead where he'd seen the stranger turn. When he whipped around the same corner their quarry had disappeared. No blazing tail lights ahead or to either side. The night seemed to have swallowed him whole.

Disorienting streets made a quick search of the area ineffective. McAllister thought he'd done a good job of tailing the suspect but now he had a feeling the stranger might have realized he was being followed. The only solution was to head home. When they collapsed in bed the neon numbers on the clock read almost two; Tanya curled tightly against Michael spoon style.

"At least we went out for a drink tonight, almost like a date."

"You're the one who wanted to get into the detective business."

Chapter 19

McAllister called Palatine the next morning, suggesting a meeting in the first person.

"Tanya and I followed Reed last night. He met with an unidentified man at a place in Santa Cruz called the Red Parrott."

"I know the place. You say an unidentified man?"

"We never got a good look at him. We followed him to Monterey then lost him."

Palatine removed a legal sized folder from a briefcase sitting beside his desk. He opened it and slid a page across the desk.

"Could this be the man Reed met?"

McAllister looked at the photo.

"No. The man I saw was short and stocky. He didn't have long hair like this. Who's this guy?"

"He's the guy who bled all over the De Costa's kitchen, the possibly late Clarence Waters. I'd like you to go down to the Red Parrot and show his picture around to the staff. See if anyone recognizes him. If you get lucky, see what you can find out about who he was hanging around with. You said Reed had a distinctive look; bright red hair, right? See if Reed and Waters were seen together. I think the fact that Reed went there last night might mean he's been using it as a meeting place."

"I'll be down there by lunch."

The chief had one more order for McAllister before the detective got up from his chair. "This might be the break we've been waiting for. We need to get together with De Costa tomorrow. I want to be the one to tell him we got an I.D. on the blood. I'll call you and let you know when and where."

McAllister was already driving the shit-mobile so he was ready for action. A detective uniform consisting of a Tommy Bahama shirt, faded blue jeans, boots, sun glasses and baseball cap insured he would remain incognito. Retracing his path down the Santa Cruz Highway from the night before, he made a quick call to check in with Tanya. When he arrived the lunch crowd was grazing at full speed. A BLT and diet drink seemed in order. The Red Parrot didn't feel the need to stock Diet Dr. Pepper so the detective had to grit his teeth with a substitute. The club had been transformed into a sleepy little tourist trap in the daylight. The waitress seemed very young but McAllister decided he might as well start with her. When she delivered his sandwich he showed her Water's picture and asked if she had seen him before.

"Are you a cop?"

"I'm a private detective."

"You're pretty cute for a detective."

"A modeling agency in Los Angeles decides who gets to be a detective." She laughed, which was his goal. "This is serious. I'm working on a case. I need to know if you've seen this guy in here." She concentrated on the picture for a minute but finally shook her head. "Can I speak to your manager?"

"Sure, her name is Carol. I'll go get her."

McAllister repeated the story for Carol who proved to be a little more helpful, showing the picture to the rest of the staff working lunch. She returned with a good idea.

"No luck but there's a different crew for evenings and weekends. You should try after six."

"I'll do that. Thanks for your help. Please keep this quiet."

A Coca-Cola clock high on the wall signaled a little after one. With some time to kill he drove around the bay to look at the Jack Waldorf monument at Lighthouse Point. On the way back he took a chance and rang the bell at Buck Snider's house. When Buck answered the detective was surprised by his appearance. Snider had deteriorated noticeably during the past year. An enthusiastic hand shake sent a message the old man wasn't getting many visitors. McAllister guessed age had put Buck under house arrest.

Looking over McAllister's shoulder he calmly appraised the detective's new ride. "Why in the hell are you driving that piece of junk?"

"It's on loan from the Los Gatos Police Department. I'm nosing around on a case. I can't use Lucille because she would draw too much attention. This thing's invisible. By the way, do you know the official definition of a shit-mobile?"

"The car you're driving would qualify based on any set of criteria. Come inside and I'll get you something to drink."

McAllister used the opportunity to pick Buck's brain on another matter that had been bothering him. "May I ask you a few more questions about Jack Waldorf? Everything you've told me made him out as such a fascinating person. I find it a little eerie living in his house."

"What would you like to know?"

"I can't get my mind around how such an obviously wealthy bachelor could live above the garage in the little suite. Why wouldn't he get his own place? I would think he'd be living in something pretty fancy."

"The answer is simple. Two reasons, really. First, and most important, he promised his mother he would live on the estate with her. Remember, she was living in a grand mansion in England. When her husband was killed, she wanted Jack to move back and run the business but he would have no part of it. Jack persuaded his mother to sell the family's holdings and move to California. His promise to live at the estate sealed the deal."

"Why didn't he want to run the business?"

"It's probably impossible for your generation to fully appreciate how the war changed us. Jack knew any day he got in his Spitfire might be his last. He witnessed so many of the men he knew get killed, blasted to pieces in mid-air, crashing in a ball of fire. No man can sit behind a desk after that."

"You managed to adjust pretty well."

"I just repaired the planes when they brought them back. I wasn't getting shot at. It was different for me."

"You said two reasons."

"Jack loved racing that C-type Jag more than anything in the world. The old Jag was the closest thing he could find to flying the Spitfire. He had an idea he could be a professional driver, although in truth he wasn't quite as good as the best. Money wasn't an issue as much as he just needed something to keep him busy. He longed for that adrenaline rush. He loved living down at the garage with his cars."

"What about women?"

"What about them?"

"I mean Jack Waldorf. How could he live in that little garage and entertain women."

"Jack could have any woman he wanted. I remember many times during the war we'd spend the evening in a bar having drinks. I spent most of my time chasing the women. We found plenty of them and top of the line, too. Jack would ignore them until it was time to leave then he'd simply nod at one and take her home effortlessly. Women were not a problem for Jack."

"He'd take them back to the garage?"

"They'd go with him anywhere. Jack probably had a few of them in your old Jag."

McAllister hadn't considered that possibly but continued, "Never anyone special?"

"Near the end there was a girl. I think he wanted kids, especially for his mother's sake. Jack kind of let it slip he was going to pop the question shortly before he got killed."

"The news must have been devastating. What happened to the girl?"

"I lost track of her. I think I remember she got married shortly after Jack died. She didn't seem to want to see us anymore. Too many memories I guess." McAllister loved the old guy. Listening to war stories made time stand still but he eventually noticed the sun was getting close to the water. After a heartfelt farewell to Buck he returned to the club on the wharf. As McAllister entered the bar, he decided to sit near the railing where he had seen Reed meet the other man. When his waitress arrived he repeated his earlier routine with the picture.

"You're the detective?"

"What do you mean?"

"Carol told us you might be by as she was leaving her shift. She also said you talk like a cowboy." Suzy, that was the waitress' name, looked carefully at Water's picture. "Yeah, I've seen this guy in here plenty of times. Four of them would come in; two just last night. Come to think of it, this one wasn't with the others the last few times."

"What about a man with bright red curly hair? Was he part of the group?"

"Yeah. This guy in the picture, the one with the red hair and two others."

"What do the other two guys look like?"

"One of them is scary; not very tall, a little overweight but the way he would stare at me just gave me the creeps. He was here last night with the red-headed guy."

"What about the other one?"

"All-American boy with blue eyes, blond hair. Really good looking."

"Can you possibly remember if they paid with a credit card last night? I'm working on an important case and a name would be a big help."

"Sorry. They always paid in cash. I remember because they were good tippers."

McAllister gave her one of Palatine's cards and asked her to call if any of them showed up again.

"You want me to give your number to Carol?"

"She hadn't seen these guys before. I think they just come by in the evenings."

"No, I mean personally. She thinks you're hot for an old guy."

Her comment left McAllister speechless so he pulled out a twenty and gave it to her for his drink.

Chapter 20

Chief Palatine's admin peeked in the door shortly after ten the next morning.

"Wilson didn't show up for work this morning. He's not answering his cell phone, either."

The chief found the information surprising, considering Wilson's dedication to his job.

"I'll drop by his house and make sure everything's okay. I'm sure he has a good explanation."

The drive only took a few minutes. The chief noted Wilson's truck was missing as he pulled up. Still hoping nothing was amiss; the police officer in him wondered if he should play it tough or easy? Charlene made the choice for him when she answered the door. Normally quite an attractive woman, her hair looked like it had been brushed once as an afterthought. No makeup. Bloodshot eyes announced she hadn't slept much lately.

"Bobby's missing."

Palatine shifted into full police mode. "Since when?"

"He went out three nights ago and didn't come back. I was sure he would show up in time for work but now I know something's wrong."

Palatine pushed his way inside and closed the door behind him. Charlene led him to the main room where they both took a seat. Palatine leaned forward, eager to hear her story. "Tell me everything. Take your time and don't leave out any details."

"Bobby got a call on his cell phone. He told me he had to go out on some business. He wouldn't tell me what it was about but he seemed pretty excited. I haven't heard from him since. I'm worried because he's not answering his cell phone." She started to break down. Palatine reached across and put a steadying hand on her shoulder. "I'm scared something has happened to him." The chief kept quiet, forcing her to keep talking. "I don't know how to say this any other way so I'm just going to give it to you straight. I think Bobby has been involved in some stealing or something."

"Go on."

"We're not rich. No police officer is rich. We pay our bills okay. We don't over-extend ourselves so we have a pretty good life. In the last six months it seems like Bobby's had more money than usual; always cash. He bought me some new furniture about three months ago. A month later he brought home a big screen television as a surprise, a top-of-the-line Sony model. When I asked him about where the money came from he wouldn't give me a straight answer. A few months ago he bought an old Corvette Stingray convertible, not a show winner or anything but where'd he find the money for a sports car? I keep a close watch on our bank account so I'm sure he hasn't touched it. And that's not all."

"What else?"

"I have a brother. He's been in some trouble. He just got out of prison last year after he got caught with some stolen jewelry. Bobby offered to help him find work. I don't know what they worked out but he's been doing much better lately; that is until he disappeared." She looked up from her Kleenex at the chief's unwavering stare. He still didn't offer anything. "I haven't heard from him in over three weeks. I drove over to his place and the mail was piled up in his mailbox. The house looked deserted."

"Does he live in Santa Cruz?"

Her face turned white; proving Palatine had guessed correctly.

"How did you know that?"

"We've got a lot more talking to do. I need you to come with me to the station and make a statement. You'll need to fill out a couple of missing persons reports. Do you want a lawyer present?"

"A lawyer?"

"I'm afraid you might need one."

For the first time Palatine knew for sure one of his men was involved in the De Costa killings. He remembered Wilson's fingerprints in the house. Now he knew he hadn't messed up investigating the crime scene. Wilson was in the house the night the De Costas were kidnapped. Reed, Waters and now Wilson. Waters and Wilson probably dead. The fourth man? Palatine's bet was on Monroe.

121

Chapter 21

Michael and Tanya were invited to a meeting at Blue's house at nine that evening. The chief led the discussion.

"The blood in the kitchen doesn't match either of your parents, Blue. It did, however, match an ex-con named Clarence Waters, who lived in Santa Cruz."

"I've never heard of him. What would his blood be doing in our house?"

"I think he was in on the crime. I think he got himself hurt in the process. I used an operative to look around a house he'd been renting to see if anything would turn up."

"Did he find anything?"

"The box contained about three weeks' worth of mail. The date on the oldest bill was close to the time your parents disappeared. I don't think we'll be meeting up with him in the present tense. His blood at your house proves he was involved in your parents' murders; I just couldn't fill in the blanks of where it all started and how it progressed from your house to the ranch. That is, until today." He paused for a deep breath. "One of my officers, Wilson, went missing three nights ago. I think he's in on this, too."

Now McAllister couldn't connect the dots. "Why do you think he's part of it?"

"Wilson's wife's name is Charlene, whose brother just happens to be the same Clarence Waters. Wilson found him some work when he got out of prison that seemed to have been profitable."

"You think Wilson is in the past tense, too?"

"He would've contacted his wife by now."

Now it was McAllister's turn to talk. "I already told the chief about this but I'll repeat it for you, Blue. We tailed Reed to the Red Parrot Friday night. He met a guy there but we couldn't I.D. him. We managed to follow him to Monterey but lost him. The next day the chief gave me a picture of Waters to show around. Waters was seen several times over the past few months, but not lately. A waitress at the Red Parrot reported she saw four men meet on a regular basis. Waters and Reed were two of them. I know Reed was one of them because he's easy to identify with his bright red hair. I met Wilson here the night we tested for the blood evidence. He matched the description of another man described by a witness as meeting with the group."

The chief stewed a minute then decided to share.

"I'd be willing to bet the fourth man is Monroe. I'll be able to confirm it as soon as I can get a man back down to the Red Parrott with Wilson and Monroe's pictures. Now we know the identities of the men we think murdered your parents. The next question is what were they after? I don't have a good answer, yet."

McAllister had been chewing on an idea for several days. Now seemed like a good time to share. "Chief, I've got an idea. You probably won't like it."

"Listening doesn't cost much."

The detective paused a moment and looked at his girl before he started. She was still gorgeous, just like every other day of her life. "I'm not a patient man. I don't like waiting around for the bad guys to make each move. I think I know a way for us to get ahead of them." First, Blue, do you still have those contracts from Reed in your safe?"

"Absolutely."

"Okay. This is what I'm thinking. Call Reed in the morning around ten and tell him it's no deal then hang up real quick. Don't give him a chance to ask you any questions. Chief, you drive down to his office so you can be ready right after the phone call. Blue, you call the chief on his cell phone as soon as you hang up with Reed. Chief, as soon as Blue calls, you pay Reed a visit. Question him for about an hour. Shake him up. Throw out a few tidbits and let him try to explain things. Basically scare the shit out of him but, you know, in a professional way.

"I'm going to be outside Reed's house when you start. You call me on my cell just before you shake down Reed. I'm going to give his house a look. I should have a good hour at least. Plenty of time. Chief, you can call me if anything goes wrong. When you're done head downstairs and wait to see if Reed runs to Monroe."

Tanya piped in. "I'm going with you, Michael, but won't we need a search warrant?"

All eyes turned to the chief. "I think we're past that now. If you find something you'll have to leave it there but we'll know where to find it if we come back, legal like."

Chapter 22

McAllister liked being on the offensive. At ten he and Tanya were parked in the shit-mobile a block from Patrick Reed's house. Fifteen minutes later they got the call. Chief Palatine confirmed Blue had called Reed and he was ready to move in. Tanya seemed excited by the prospect of breaking and entering.

"I knew you'd open new doors for me but I never expected anything like this."

"Nothing but the best for you, princess. It's only taken me a year to turn you into a full-fledged criminal."

An alley behind the houses led to Reed's garage about half way down the block. The neighborhood was in the old part of town with houses framed by mature trees and bushes. As long as no one happened to drive up the alley they could approach without being seen. The back gate was unlocked, revealing a small, older bungalow. An alarm system didn't put up much of a fight.

"What other illicit skills have you been hiding from me?"

"This is all in the detective books. You'll have to do some studying if you want to get your license."

His trusty pocket knife did its work on the door. After a couple of minutes the lock gave up, welcoming them into the kitchen. The curtains were already drawn on the front of the house, allowing them to work without being seen from the street.

"Let's take a walk through the house. A quick look will tell us how we should proceed."

The place seemed newly refurbished, two bedrooms and a bath with a brand new kitchen. The bath also had the smell of a freshly done project. One bedroom was just that, the other was an office. The office contained a desk and two large metal filing cabinets but no computer.

"Reed must have everything on a lap top. I'll have a look through the rest of the house. Run through the files and see if you can find anything that looks like it's tied to De Costa."

McAllister walked back to the main bedroom. He tossed each drawer of the dresser first but found nothing out of the norm. The night stands contained a few papers but nothing interesting. No guns. McAllister guessed Reed relied on others for muscle. A smallish walk-in closet was neatly arranged with clothes tagged with nice labels. McAllister noticed things like that. He searched under a rug and behind all the pictures but couldn't find a safe. The rest of the house didn't reveal anything very interesting.

When the detective returned to the second bedroom he found Tanya leaning over the desk going through papers, showing off her rather perfect ass in a particularly lewd manner. When he moved up behind her she swayed against him seductively and purred.

"Something's kind of got me excited." He moved his arms around her waist, then up, cupping each breast in a hand. She turned to her left and kissed him hard and wet on the mouth. He slid his hands down, his fingers finding their way inside her jeans on each side. She unzipped them and allowed him to push them down around her knees, catching her panties with them. She crossed her fore arms on the desk and braced her head. "I need it hard this time."

For the next ten or fifteen minutes, McAllister wasn't able to make a good estimate of the time, they accomplished nothing in the way of detective work on the De Costa case. Something about breaking the law seemed to really got Tanya hot. The most explosive sex they'd ever enjoyed left him panting over her when it was time to resume their search.

"Did you find anything useful in the files?"

"No, but I'm really glad you brought me along on the investigation."

Slightly embarrassed but not sorry, Michael tried to steer them back to the main reason for their larceny.

"I was sure he'd have a safe but I can't find it. We'd better get out of here."

After a bit of tidying up by each of them in the bathroom, McAllister relocked the back door and pulled it shut. As they were walking to the gate he thought of the garage just as the chief called on his cell phone.

"I rattled him pretty good. I haven't had that much fun in a long time. I'm going to watch his car for a few minutes. He might do something stupid."

"We're finished with the house. I'm afraid we came up empty. I'm going to check the garage on our way out."

The lock on the garage door was in critical condition. A single window provided plenty of illumination. A safe cemented into the floor on one side was absolutely the only item in the entire structure.

"I can't do anything with this now but it's good to know where it is. Maybe all the files on De Costa are hidden inside. The police can come back with a search warrant if it comes to that."

They both breathed a sigh of relief when they returned to the invisibility of the shit-mobile. McAllister was used to undercover work but for Tanya it was a first.

"Well, I learned one thing today for sure." McAllister was interested in what she might have found constructive in their assignment. "Detective work is pure sex. I'm never going to allow you to work with a female partner. I'm also thinking how great it's going to be the next time I have lunch with the girls."

"You can't tell them what we've been doing."

"Are you kidding? No one has ever had a story this good. I'll leave out enough details so we won't get in trouble."

Chief Palatine called again later in the day.

"We started the ball rolling. After I left Reed's office I waited down the street to see if he would run. He didn't leave but he did come out a few minutes later to make a cell phone call. He stood by his car and seemed to be having a heated conversation. I think I scared him pretty well."

McAllister related the information on the safe in the garage. Otherwise, it seemed Reed's house was clean.

Chapter 23

Michael and Tanya shared a few minutes at breakfast before she headed for San Francisco, making a big production about business meetings during the day. Michael figured she'd arranged a lunch with her best girlfriends.

Alone, he immediately fretted about the case. He couldn't shake a strange feeling of impending doom; the warning by Tanya's mother about keeping her daughter safe running in a continuous loop through his mind. Reed and Monroe had to know the police were closing in. Only a couple of morons would think they were in the clear. McAllister didn't think Reed would be much of a problem to arrest but Monroe was a different matter. As a detective, he'd be carrying a gun and would know how to use it. A cell phone ring provided a welcome distraction. Palatine belted a request that sounded a lot more like an order.

"I need you to get over here pronto."

Over here was a neighborhood on the south side of Los Gatos. Upon arrival he found two police cars and the chief's truck. Quickly parking a block away he hustled as he approached the scene. Two officers he didn't recognize were stringing yellow tape to keep bystanders away. Stacy Carson was investigating an old car, a Chevy he thought. She gave him a nod and resumed her work. Palatine waved him over.

"I got a call from two sets of parents two days ago. I was sure we had a couple of run-away lovers. A neighbor reported the girl's car this morning. It's been parked here for several days according to a witness. I'd like you to look at it and tell me what you think."

McAllister didn't hesitate. Carson seemed to know what had been discussed and moved away for a minute, giving the detective full access of the car. As soon as he approached the open window his nose was assaulted by the nauseating smell of blood. He immediately noted a huge amount of it spewed across the car starting on the seat and windshield near the steering wheel and extending across to the other side of the car, but it was more than just blood. Human tissue was too obvious to miss, most likely brain matter but he wasn't going to make a guess. Long strands of hair on the far side of the dashboard reinforced the brain matter idea. One area on the far door wasn't bloody. His eyes soaked up the scene for a minute and then he walked back to the chief so Stacy could get back to work.

"I'd say the driver got shot in the head from close range. The shooter was standing at the window but it was down because I didn't see any glass on the seat. Makes me think the driver might have known who fired the shots. Someone was sitting in the rider's seat because the door was not covered in blood. Part of the blood spatter landed on whoever was sitting there. My guess is if you have two young lovers missing, they're both dead."

"Why do you say both dead?"

"Whoever shot the driver wouldn't let the other one get away. How could the local residents miss this?"

"This little cul-de-sac kind of kept it hidden. The owner of the corner house was out of town so it took a few days until someone finally strolled by and looked inside. Can you follow me back to the station for a few minutes?" The statement wasn't a question.

The chief met him in his office.

"Damn. I've been the chief here for eight years. We've never had anything serious happen. Now, it looks like we've got a mass murderer on the loose."

"I assume you've called the parents?"

"They're on their way down. I wanted a minute before I had to deal with them. By the way, do you have your gun with you?"

"No. It's buried somewhere in my stuff at home. I can find it easily enough."

"So if a bad guy showed up with a gun, he could just walk right up and shoot you?"

"You have a point."

"I want you carrying a gun immediately until the case is over. I'm short-handed with Wilson out of the picture. I'm going to need all the help I can get."

"You think Reed and Monroe are going to try something?"

"I'm not taking any chances from here on in. I can't picture these kids being involved with Reed and Monroe so maybe something else is going on, too. I'm going to prepare for anything."

"I'd say just the opposite. No murders for eight years and then all of these at once. They're related all right. You just don't know how."

As soon as he arrived home, McAllister dug out his gun and shoulder holster along with a heavily worn shoe box from the packing boxes shipped from Oklahoma a year earlier. Sitting by the pool with his favorite soft drink he spent an hour thoroughly cleaning and oiling his six inch Smith and Wesson 38. The next step was to load it with bullets designed to drop a bad guy with the first shot. Replacing it in the holster, he wrapped the belt tightly around the gun and walked out to the shit-mobile. Removing the keys from his pocket he opened the trunk and wedged the gun near the right tail light, standard procedure from his days with the police. When he returned to his make shift work shop he found a smaller gun in the cleaning box. He repeated the cleaning process then rolled up his right pant leg and strapped the small gun to his ankle.

Chapter 24

McAllister sat at the bar in the kitchen watching Tanya while she made dinner, grinning and chuckling to herself the whole time. Apparently she'd reached superstar status among her friends.

McAllister decided to change her thought pattern. "The manager at the Red Parrot thinks I'm hot for an old guy."

She laughed so hard she almost dropped the salad bowl.

"For what it's worth I think you're hot, too, for an old guy."

"I have some good news. I'm practically working for the city of Los Gatos, temporarily at least. Palatine says he needs my help with Wilson gone."

"Can you do anything about our electric bill?"

Michael ignored her remark.

"The chief and I had a little talk. I'm almost like a Special Investigator."

"Is he going to issue you a gun?" A short silence ensued.

"As a matter of fact he insisted I start carrying my old gun. I spent some time this afternoon getting it ready."

Tanya quit joking when she heard his response.

"You've got a gun? Where is it?"

"It's in the trunk of the shit-mobile so I don't shoot myself."

"I want to see it."

"You're kidding, right?"

"No, I really want to see it. I can't believe you're going to be packing heat. Dinner can warm up on the stove for a few minutes. Come on, hurry. Are you going to wear it under your jacket like Blue's men do?"

Her comments caught McAllister off guard. He'd kept his gun hidden when he shipped his belongings to California, assuming she'd be horrified by the sight of it. They strolled out to the car with the cicadas singing loudly in the background. He opened the trunk and showed her the weapon. Of course she wanted to hold it. Carefully removing the speed cylinder, he handed it to her. She aimed it around at the trees. Luckily no squirrels were in the act of committing crimes. They would've been dead meat, if the gun had been loaded of course.

"I can't believe how heavy it is. I've never held a gun before."

"You definitely have to get used to it. I need to go to the range as soon as I can."

"Can I go, too?"

"You want to learn how to shoot a gun?"

"I think it would be cool to go to a range with you."

"Okay. I'll take you when we get some time. It's probably not the worst idea in the world for you to be able to shoot a gun."

"If I were going to shoot somebody how would I do it? Would I try to shoot the gun out of the bad guy's hands?"

"Only if you were an actress filming a movie. Hitting anything with a pistol is pretty difficult unless you're very close. My advice would be to hold your arms straight out, lock your elbows and aim right at the middle of your target. Let go with three or four shots on the chance one of them might actually hit something. Usually the sound of the damn thing is enough to make the crooks run for their lives. And by the way, your ears would ring for a day."

"Why would I want to lock my elbows?"

"Believe it or not, this little gun kicks like a mule. Your first shot might be close but the second one would probably be aimed at the treetops or the back of the gun might hit you in the teeth."

"You know, I just thought of something. Like I said, I might be having another lunch with the girls next week. Is there any way I could borrow your gun and take it with me, just to show off a little?"

"I thought you had a business meeting today?"

Tanya watched carefully as he rewound the holster around the gun and replaced it exactly as it was before.

"Why are you wedging it back there like that?"

"I don't want it rolling around while I'm driving."

"Why do you keep it loaded?"

"If I do need it, I'll need it ready to use. I keep the safety off so don't ever touch it. It's a double action model so that's the only safety I use."

"What's a double action?"

"A double action gun must have the hammer pulled back before it can fire. Therefore, if you drop it accidentally, it can't go off. When you pull the trigger it pulls the hammer back first and then releases it. It's safer than a single action gun."

Michael told her about the bloody car when they returned to the house for dinner which resulted in more questions from his new partner. The local papers would undoubtedly sensationalize the latest murders. Something had been bouncing around in McAllister's mind all day. He decided to try it on Tanya.

"If you had to guess, do you think the Monterey detective is the brains of the outfit or Reed, the business guy?"

Tanya seemed to consider his question for a minute before answering.

"I'd have to see more of Reed in action. I mean, I haven't even heard him speak. I think I'd have to see how he handled himself around the others to figure out who was in charge. I didn't get any kind of vibe when we saw them at the Red Parrot but we were pretty far away."

"Well, they'll both be behind bars soon. The cops will figure it out. At the rate they're disappearing, there might not be much of the gang left pretty soon."

McAllister decided to give the case a rest. Once they finished picking at dinner, the couple moved into the den but didn't turn on the television. Tanya sat on Michael's lap in his favorite over-sized leather chair.

"Do you know what the most important characteristic of a girlfriend is?"

"Outstanding sex?"

"No."

"Not sex? I guess I have no idea then."

"She has to be a great snuggler."

Tanya moved in even closer with her arms around his neck, gently kissing him.

"So how do I rate?"

"World class."

He estimated they were the happiest two people on planet earth at that moment. He turned when he heard the door squeak near the kitchen but before he could make a move a man entered the house with a gun pointed directly at them. His build resembled the man they'd seen Patrick Reed meet at the Red Parrot.

"Well, look at the love birds. Get up slowly and keep your hands where I can see them."

They did as he suggested. The stranger quickly and expertly checked McAllister to see if he had a gun. Obviously he had some experience doing that sort of thing but McAllister had hidden the small gun on his ankle well. Tanya took a step away while

Michael was searched. McAllister noticed her eyes glued to the gun.

"You're getting to be a pain in the ass, McAllister. I've decided I've had enough of you. Unfortunately that's not good news for your girlfriend."

McAllister knew he only needed an instant to get to his back-up gun. If this stranger was going to kill them at the house he would have done it already. He had to be planning to take them somewhere else. The bad guy knew McAllister was the main threat and kept his eyes on the detective every second. Why in the hell hadn't he installed a better security system?

"If you're going to get rid of us, why don't you answer a few questions?"

"That kind of dialogue never works for the bad guys, McAllister. Get outside. We're going for a ride." He waved his gun at the open door.

McAllister was relieved to see only the shit-mobile in the moon light. Monroe must have walked up from the creek. A new security system might not have stopped him. He kept the gun on McAllister continuously.

"Toss the keys to the girl. This is how it's going to be. You're both getting in the trunk. The girl first."

Tanya did as she was told. After unlocking the trunk lid, she carefully stepped in and lay down along the far side of the trunk.

McAllister watched her hands to make sure she knew what to do. Monroe kept his attention, and the gun, on McAllister.

"Now you."

McAllister took two steps away from the car to give Tanya a couple more seconds to get ready, giving the tough guy an inquisitive look. "I have a bad feeling about this. I think you might shoot us both when we're in the trunk."

"I'm telling you for the last time, cut out the funny business. Get in the trunk or I'll shoot you where you stand."

Instead, McAllister took one more step back from the car. "You ever have a girlfriend, Monroe? One who would do anything in the world to save your life?"

Confused, he finally turned his gaze toward Tanya. A beautiful blonde kneeling in the trunk with arms extended and elbows locked was the last thing he ever saw. Tanya gave him a lesson in loyalty he'd never forget. A former tough guy dropped like a bag of sand. McAllister was on him like a cat but it didn't make any difference because he was probably dead before he hit the ground. Tanya would probably have fired two or three more shots as he had instructed but the kick of the gun knocked her backwards, smacking her head hard on the trunk lid. McAllister scooped the gun from the floor of the trunk and opened the cylinder.

"Is he?"

"Yes. You're a fast learner, princess."

McAllister flipped open his cell phone and called Palatine on his direct line, finding him at home.

"Tanya and I just had some trouble at our house. One of our suspects broke in with some bad intentions."

"Are you okay?"

"We are. The bad guy isn't."

"I'll have the troops there in five minutes."

McAllister took a minute to inspect the dead man. His jacket pockets undoubtedly contained an ID but he decided he'd have enough explaining to do without adding his fingerprints to the victim's body. When the chief arrived he answered an important question pronto.

"Monroe, right?"

"Yeah. This proves he's been in on this from the start. I don't get why he came after you, though."

Michael and Tanya were taken to separate rooms for grilling. Chief Palatine took no chances and followed protocol to the letter, only releasing them after an hour of questioning.

"I think that'll do for tonight. I won't have any trouble finding you if I need more information."

Six hours after the shooting the police finished recording evidence at the scene and removed the shit-mobile along with McAllister's gun; leaving the house suddenly quiet. Michael took Tanya in his arms, holding her for a long time in a close embrace.

"Will they arrest Reed now?"

"Probably already have."

"I can't stay here anymore."

"What do you mean?"

"I'll never be able to forget this. I'll never feel safe here. I want to move back to Peter's house. I wish we could go right now."

He could see the whole thing starting to hit her as the blood drained from her face. Suddenly she ran for the bathroom. He rubbed her back while she threw up in the toilet. After a minute she shooed him out and closed the door. Michael could hear the water running for a few minutes and when Tanya returned she'd brushed her hair and washed her face but she still seemed panicked.

"Michael, what's happened to our lives? Peter's gone. We'll have to have security guards follow us around all the time. I wish I'd never seen this place. It's cursed. It killed Jack Waldorf and it almost killed us."

He pulled her into his lap again on the chair. He hugged her and rubbed her back to try to calm her. "If you want to move back to town, that's fine with me. Let's sleep on it. Decide in the morning what you want to do."

"I put so much work into this house. I wanted it to be our dream. Now, it's turned into a nightmare. I don't need to sleep on it. I'm driving to San Francisco in the morning. I'm going to start making plans for the move. I've got to discuss this with mother.

You don't mind if she lives with us, do you? Will you go with me?"

"Let me stay here and finish with Palatine. I want to put this De Costa case to bed so we can make a clean break."

"I want to spend the night in San Francisco. I'm scared to come back here, now more than ever."

"Do whatever you need to do. We'll talk in the afternoon and decide our next move."

"If I stay in town, you have to drive up. That's our deal."

Chapter 25

The most dangerous animal in the woods outside the old Waldorf mansion was neither a wolf nor mountain lion but rather a serial killer with a body of work stretching into a fifth decade. Tonight was show time. Years of practice allowed him to crouch motionless in thick undergrowth for long periods of time. Deer passed nearby giving him a wary look as he waited for the lights to go out at the house.

Hearing something approaching from behind, he turned slowly and silently from his cover. With two hand guns and two large knives in his possession, he wasn't worried about protecting himself, but this was a confusing development. The sound could only be human. A man appeared in a few minutes and passed within ten yards as he proceeded straight toward the house, lights blazing inside and around the pool. After checking a gun, the man hustled across the clearing to the back of the house, moving inside after a short pause. The killer had watched Michael and Tanya walk out to the car a few minutes earlier as he showed off a gun but he had returned it to the back of the car. Apparently the couple had neglected to lock the door when they went back inside.

The killer moved quickly to the edge of the clearing so he could watch the proceedings inside the house. The intruder used his gun to subdue the owners and rightfully checked the McAllister for a weapon. What was going to happen next? Was this a robbery? The answer came a few minutes later. All three emerged from the back of the house, the intruder ordering the couple into the back of the trunk of the lone car in the driveway. The killer had put in far too much work on this project to allow someone else to take his victims. He decided to kill the intruder as soon as he had a clear shot. The girl climbed into the trunk. Ah, the gun! Would she have the knowledge and courage to use it? He could hear Michael distracting the intruder. Sure enough a few seconds later Tanya managed a shot from point blank range, dropping the intruder instantly with a single shot.

When Michael pulled his cell phone the killer knew two things. First, he had to get out of the woods immediately. The police would be swarming the scene in a matter of minutes and he had a long way to go to get back to his car. Secondly, his precious plan, which had taken months to form, was ruined. He would have to come up with something completely new. No doubt the security systems on this house and the one in San Francisco would be upgraded very soon. A new plan began to form as he hurried back down to the stream.

Chapter 26

Tanya brewed a coffee the next morning then sprayed gravel as she headed out of the gate. Palatine called while the rocks were still rolling down the drive.

"Don't let your guard down. This isn't over yet."

"What in the hell do you mean by that?"

"Santa Cruz executed a search warrant on Reed's place at the same time the Monterey Police did on Monroe's place. Guess what?"

"They found everything they needed in the safe in Reed's garage."

"They found nothing at either place. I heard Monroe's place looked like it had been sanitized. Reed's missing. I think he might come after you."

"The next person who ventures on this property is going to get shot with no questions asked."

"Don't joke about it. There's still something going on."

"I'll be down at the station in a few minutes. I need to talk to you. It won't take long."

McAllister didn't waste time when he sat down across from Palatine. "I'm done with the De Costa case."

"What's up? I thought you wanted to see this thing to the end?"

"Tanya's scared to death. We came pretty close to getting ourselves killed last night. She's adamant about moving back to San Francisco and I don't blame her."

"What's about the Waldorf place? You two have gone to quite an expense to renovate the place."

"I have an idea it'll be on the market pretty soon. Her mother reamed my ass the other night about putting Tanya in danger. I can only imagine what she's going to do the next time I see her. She was right, though. I should never have involved myself in this case."

"What about Reed?"

"He won't come after us, especially after what happened to Monroe. He doesn't seem the type of guy who could handle the rough stuff, anyway. Besides, I'm pretty sure we'll have our very own army following us everywhere we go from now on. I've decided it's up to you to catch him. I don't think it'll take long."

Palatine stood and extended his hand. "Thanks for helping me. If I can help you in any way in the future, give me a call."

McAllister felt a huge weight off his shoulders when he arrived back at the Waldorf place. An ice cold Diet Dr. Pepper seemed like a great way to celebrate the end of the case. He headed upstairs to Tanya's office to investigate a book on a slightly more innocent matter. The conversation with Buck had jogged his memory about a nagging loose end. His retirement from the De Costa case lasted until his cell phone rang about two hours later.

The name on the display was Stacy Carson. Against his better judgment he answered. "McAllister."

"I need to talk to you about the De Costa case."

McAllister hung up immediately but Carson immediately called back.

"Listen, Stacy, no offense, but I don't want to talk to you. I'm off the De Costa case. I just told the chief."

"I know. I saw you at the station. I wanted to talk to you but I couldn't risk Palatine seeing us in the parking lot. Just give me five minutes. What have you got to lose?"

"I don't have time to give you a detailed answer on how much I have to lose. I assume you want to come over. When can you get here?"

"I'm outside the gate. Open up."

Pushing a button by the intercom, he walked out back. Stacy carried a folder under her arm when she got out of her car. The granite topped island in the kitchen provided a temporary office. McAllister offered her a coffee even though he wasn't sure he could work the machine. Luckily she refused.

"I still think Palatine might be mixed up in this."

The conversation had turned even worse than he'd imagined.

"I guess I have no choice but to listen, right?"

"The chief isn't following up on leads. I went to him months ago because I was sure someone on our team was dirty. I didn't think it was Wilson but I'd heard some things. He's not following up or he's doing everything on his own, secretly."

"So you've decided the worst case scenario?"

"No, but I want to get to the bottom of this. I swiped a file out of his office yesterday and copied it. There might be something we can use."

The "we" part didn't sound good. Still, the detective in McAllister couldn't resist a look at the contents of the folder. The first thing of interest was Reed's phone records.

"He said he didn't want to tap Reed's phone but this was done weeks ago. Have you tracked down any of these numbers?"

"I would've had them all done if you hadn't caused all the excitement here last night. Most of the calls were to Monroe but the others seem insignificant. Three numbers are to what I assume are clients. One of them lives very close to his house, although that one might just be his tennis partner for all I know. The other two are business numbers, contractors."

"That's all? Three unknown numbers for the last two months?"

The detective quickly jotted down part of the information on his trusty note pad then paged through the rest of the documents. The chief had been checking into Valentino De Costa a lot more than he'd let on, too. It seemed the chief considered him a stronger suspect than he led them to believe, at least initially, or possibly the chief, himself, had been involved in the murders.

"You're sure the chief doesn't know you have this?"

"Positive. What are you going to do?"

"Probably lose my mind but first I'm going to have one last look at Reed's place. Maybe something will turn up. I'll call you tomorrow from San Francisco if I find anything. We're moving back to the city."

"Your girlfriend doesn't like playing with guns?"

"Get back to the station before Palatine figures out where you are. If he catches us, he'll give us both a good spanking this time."

"Sounds like fun."

Carson gave him a sly smile as she left. Lucille was his only choice for the trip to the coast. He spent most of the drive talking to himself; a sure sign he was going crazy. McAllister parked a block away from Reed's house on the slim chance the Jag might not be associated with a break-in if he had to run for it. The alarm system had apparently been dismantled during the raid Palatine told him about. The door lock had given up completely.

McAllister almost gave up as soon as he stepped inside. Papers were strewn throughout the house. Finding a clue in the mess would take a miracle. Since it was his last day as a detective he decided to do what good detectives do. He systematically reviewed every single piece of paper in the house; finishing as it grew dark outside. Raising his arms he tried to stretch his aching back as he looked at piles of papers neatly stacked in the kitchen. Shaking his head in resignation he decided he'd given it his best shot. As he turned to leave he noticed a calendar on the wall by the back door, still showing the previous month. Lifting the page to the current month, a three week period stood out like a stop sign, high-lighted with a yellow magic marker, beginning a few days earlier and with a name and number written in ink down the middle. McAllister recognized it as one of the names on Reed's cell phone record, the guy about a block away. Why would he have a three week meeting set up on his calendar? It was a question the detective decided to answer.

McAllister was lucky to have noticed the street name when he first started surveillance of Reed's house. The second house was a block over and farther into the neighborhood. As he walked past Lucille, he stopped to retrieve a small flashlight. Arriving at the house he took some time to see if anyone appeared to be home. The darkened house looked deserted from the front walk. Bushes and trees in the alley blocked his view of the back. Entering from the rear, the door opened the first time he touched the handle. Retrieving the small gun from his ankle he stepped inside and then stood still a minute to let his eyes adjust to the dark room. A large yellow Labrador retriever came into focus first, seemingly as surprised as the detective but wagging his tail tentatively.

McAllister had owned a lab growing up on the ranch so he decided to take a chance. He knelt down and extended his hand. The dog practically smiled as he approached for a quick pat. The first order of business was to clear the house because someone had to be taking care of the dog. He tip-toed down the hall as carefully as he could, considering the floor was oak and he was wearing boots. A bedroom at the end of the hall looked empty but the bed was unmade. The lab stuck his nose underneath and started wagging his tail.

"Come out from under the bed or I'll start shooting."

An immediate commotion soon revealed a red headed body dressed only in a pair of boxer shorts.

"Don't shoot."

McAllister carefully pushed the button on the back of the flashlight and shined it directly into Reed's eyes to blind him.

"Keep your hands where I can see them. Nobody's going to care much if I use this gun on you."

The detective carefully observed a bony excuse for a body; white as a sheet and shaking in fright. Definitely unarmed.

"I'll do whatever you say. Please don't shoot me."

The dog started barking when Reed scrambled out forcing McAllister to instruct Reed to lie face down on the bed while he calmed things down.

"Do you have any guns in the house?"

"No. I don't own a gun."

"If you lie to me, I'll shoot you."

"I swear I don't have any weapons in the house." McAllister flipped the light switch. He ordered Reed to his feet and assessed him carefully. Too many cops who had been shot or stabbed by a seemingly unarmed suspect. "Who are you?"

"McAllister."

"The one who. . ."

"Yeah. That one. This gun might be small but the bullets will kill you just as dead as the big ones. They really hurt when they go in, too. Understand?" Reed nodded vehemently. "Get dressed." McAllister dialed Tanya on his cell phone while Reed fumbled into a pair of jeans and a shirt. "I'm going to be a little late getting up to San Francisco but I promise when you wake up in the morning I'll be by your side. Don't wait up for me."

"Why don't you leave now?"

"I'm getting ready to have a discussion with Patrick Reed."

"Reed? How did you find him? What's going on?"

"It's too long a story to tell right now. Reed and I are going to have a little heart to heart talk about his criminal activities these past few weeks and then I'm going to turn him in."

"I assume you have your little gun on him. If he so much as farts, shoot him."

McAllister smiled in Reed's direction.

"Good idea. I'll tell him."

He clicked the phone off before she could ask any more questions.

"Tell me what?"

"She suggested I shoot you first and then call the cops. You've got to admit the idea has some appeal. I'm trying to decide if her plan is better than mine."

"How did you find me?"

"You wrote a note on your wall calendar, dumbass." McAllister decided he was picking up some technical terms from Palatine. "What are you doing here, anyway?"

"I jog with the guy who lives here. He's on a business trip in Europe for three weeks. I promised to feed his dog. When I found out the cops were looking for me, I realized I could put my car in the garage and hide out here for a while. I forgot I wrote it on my calendar."

"What's the dog's name?"

"Fred."

"That was the best name he could come up with? Come here, Fred."

Fred seemed like he had decided to be on McAllister's side.

"Let's move to the kitchen where we can talk." McAllister motioned to the kitchen table with his pistol, which seemed to motivate Reed, and then looked for a soft drink in the refrigerator. What he found wasn't his favorite but he decided to make do. Reed wasn't thirsty. McAllister took a seat directly across a small table from Reed and gave him his hardest, unwavering stare. "What was the idea with the De Costa killings?"

"I think I need an attorney."

McAllister's gun hand lashed out across the table in a blur, catching Reed across the temple and sending him backwards over the chair. Crouching over the redhead before he had a chance to react, McAllister took a lesson from a young woman working for the Los Gatos PD and stuck the barrel of his gun deep into his captive's right nostril.

"Wrong answer." The detective grabbed Reed by his steel wool haircut, righted the chair and threw him back in front of the table. "You're either going to tell me everything I want to know or you're not leaving this house alive." He paused to let his words take effect. "I could shoot you at any time and say you resisted arrest."

Reed made a desperate plea. "I'll get killed for sure if I talk to you."

"Are you worried about Monroe?"

"You know about Monroe?"

"Monroe came after me and my girlfriend last night. He would've killed us but he made a big mistake. You see, I don't mind people trying to kill me so much, but when they bother my girlfriend, I get mad. Really mad. I promise Monroe is no longer a threat to you. So, let's start over. What was the idea with the De Costa killings?"

"Is Monroe in jail?"

"Monroe's dead. He took one of my favorite bullets in his heart." It didn't seem possible but Reed turned even whiter. McAllister wanted to scare him out of as much information as possible because he knew this would be his only chance. Reed bowed his head and seemed to take a second to compose himself.

"I went to the Red Parrott about eight months ago. I'd been trying to finalize a real estate deal with Enrico De Costa but he was driving me nuts. De Costa would always listen but he would never commit. I finally realized he was playing me, you know, just trying to find out what my plan was for developing the property so he could steal my idea. I was pissed off so I had a few beers. A guy sat down at the bar next to me. He started buying and I started blabbing. I guess I shot my mouth off about the real estate deal."

"Monroe, right?"

"Yeah, Monroe. Before I knew it, he decided we should be partners. He implied he might have some dirt on De Costa or something like that. Maybe we could work an angle. I was drunk enough to believe him. Before I knew it Monroe had cut himself in on the whole deal."

"Explain your plan to me. I could never understand how you figured it would work."

McAllister took a second and did a visual check for a full three hundred and sixty degrees. This was the part in a movie where the good guy doesn't notice somebody sneaking up from behind. McAllister had seen that movie. Reed kept his eyes on the gun.

"We were trying to get some leverage on De Costa so we could force him sell us the land; make the deal legitimate. We thought he might have a mistress or something so we could black-mail him. The problem was Monroe couldn't find anything on him. Then he came up with a new plan to kidnap his wife."

"That's when you should've gone to the police."

"He was the police. He told me if I didn't work with him he'd kill me. He had another cop working with him, too. I couldn't go to the police."

"If you had, you wouldn't be in this spot now. Tell me what happened the night they got murdered. I want to know everything in detail. Don't leave anything out and don't lie to me, either, or I'll shoot some of your fingers off."

Reed pulled his hands back in a reflex motion. "It started early that morning."

Chapter 27

"Monroe called and told me to meet him and his men at a café in Salinas. He said we were going on a hunting trip. It occurred to me they had given up on extorting De Costa and they might have decided to drive me out in the country and shoot me but I couldn't figure a way out.

"Monroe had two men in his employ. The three of them had their own business enterprises, none of them quite within the law. These jobs did, however, seem profitable because they were habitually throwing money around; always cash. Monroe dropped rumors he'd murdered a few unfortunates along the way. I wasn't sure if it was just part of the plan to keep me off balance but I believed him."

"Wilson and Waters."

"You know about them, too?" McAllister didn't answer at first and let Reed shift uneasily in his chair.

"Don't worry about how or what I know, just keep talking."

"After breakfast we left the café in Monroe's truck, one of those big, dual wheeled jobs, and headed inland. The others were laughing at me the whole time. I guess I couldn't shake the thought I was going to get killed."

McAllister shifted in his chair, mostly due to boredom. Reed's self-pity disgusted the detective. "I get Monroe scared you. Save the dramatics and get on with your story."

"After what seemed like an hour we arrived at a ranch owned by the De Costa family. Monroe stuck to his story about hunting; entering through a gate about a half a mile down from the main one. A flimsy chain was strung through a notch so it was easy to get in. We drove another thirty minutes, finally stopping at kind of a high point over-looking a valley with a stream at the bottom."

McAllister was losing patience. "I'm getting bored. I said I wanted details but not your life story. Get to the point."

"As soon as we piled out of the truck, Wilson said he noticed something down by the stream. A set of binoculars they'd apparently brought to use in the hunt came in handy to check out a truck about a half a mile away. Wilson trained the field glasses at the truck for a minute then he handed them to Monroe for confirmation.

"Wilson had recognized three Latino boys by the truck they were driving, drug dealers from Watsonville. After watching them a while the lawmen decided they were cooking a batch of meth."

"Sounds to me like they were going to shoot you but the Latinos distracted them. No way to know for sure."

"Monroe seemed to go into a trance. I swear he sat there for five minutes just looking down the valley. Then, suddenly, he jumped up and said something about everything was perfect.

"Right then and there he outlined his plan. The drug dealers had presented an opportunity but there wasn't a minute to waste. Monroe confirmed with Wilson that Wednesday night was when Valentino drove to San Jose to party with the frat boys. I had no idea they'd had the De Costas under close surveillance. They decided to make their move that night because Valentino wouldn't be around to interfere so we hustled back down the mountain. Monroe never let me out of his sight once the plan was in motion. He followed me from the café to my house so I could change clothes and then we drove in his truck to Monterey. We waited outside De Costa's office until we saw his receptionist leave. We dropped in unannounced as soon as she drove away."

McAllister felt like he was finally getting somewhere. The Latino connection and the murder site were completely the result of a chance sighting of the meth lab operation on the De Costa ranch. "Explain Monroe's plan."

Chapter 28

Usually the decisions regarding De Costa's business were taken with careful consideration but this time was different. Replacing the gun in the drawer De Costa quickly signed two sets of original contracts while he tried to figure out his next move. Was there any way to deal with these men without bringing harm to his wife?

"You have what you want. Now leave me alone and let my wife go."

The stranger spoke with a smirk on his face.

"I'm afraid it's not going to be quite that simple. First, where would you file a contract like this?"

"Here in the office safe."

The stranger drew a gun as soon as De Costa put his down. The barrel motioned toward the contracts lying on the desk. The safe was hidden by a large picture behind the desk. Enrico spun the dial until it surrendered with a loud click, then tossed one of the two original contracts inside, closed the safe and returned the picture. Reed's briefcase took possession of the second agreement.

"Now what?"

Reed's part of the meeting seemed over. All the orders started coming from the tough guy.

"You're coming with us. If you do exactly as I say, there's a slim chance you'll survive this. If we don't show up where we're supposed to be in the next few minutes like best friends, your wife is dead. Don't try anything stupid. I always wanted to ride in a new Ferrari. You drive and I'll keep you company." He tossed a set of keys to Reed. "Follow us in my truck.

"Where am I going?"

"To your house."

De Costa's mind focused on the small gun he knew his wife carried in her apron pocket, a

practice they agreed to the day after they were married thirty years earlier. A second was all he would need to get off a couple of well-placed shots. A button on the dashboard opened the far door to the garage. He noticed Reed park the truck in the drive.

"Everyone inside." Enrico watched for an opening but the stranger never took his gun away as they ascended the stairs from the garage up to the main living area. Another stranger held a gun on his wife seated at the kitchen table on the other side of the living room. Denise ran to his arms as soon as she saw Enrico. When he kissed her he noticed an angry red welt across her forehead.

"You bastards. I did what you asked. Why did you harm my wife?"

Reed seemed stunned.

"What happened?"

"Look in here." The third man motioned around the corner into the kitchen. A man lay flat on this back, his shirt dark and wet over his heart and his body framed by a large pool of blood on the floor. The tough guy laughed.

"What happened to Clarence? Did he shoot himself?"

"No, this bitch shot him with a little tiny gun she had hidden in her apron. Clarence never knew what hit him." "I'd have saved a bullet for you if I had known there were two of you."

The unexpected development required additional consideration by the boss. "Imagine, getting shot by a woman. Okay, here's what we do. Pat, you go down and get a tarp out of the back of the truck. Help Wilson get Clarence wrapped up so he doesn't spill blood all over the place. Carry him down the stairs and stash him in the back of the truck, but you know, reverently." Still grinning he continued to spit out orders. "I'll have to think of a good place to dump him. Enrico you sit here at the table. Denise, find some bath towels and clean up the blood. When you're done put them in the washer and start it. If you try anything I'll splatter your husband's brains all over your nice curtains." In a few minutes everyone had accomplished their various tasks. "Okay. I've been thinking about this for a few minutes. De Costa, I'm going to have to charge you something for killing one of my men. What do you think is a fair price?"

"Just tell me what you want."

"I'm going to hazard a wild guess that you have a safe hidden somewhere in the house. I'm going to go way out on a limb and surmise you've got some cash in it. Let's go see if I'm right. Bobby will keep your wife company while we take care of our business."

Losing Denise's gun was a devastating set-back but Enrico's mind immediately focused on other guns hidden throughout the house. The more he could move around, the better chance he would have to get his hands on one. The safe in the basement yielded well over one hundred thousand dollars, earned tax free from gambling and gun sales over the past few years.

"Throw the money on the table over there. I don't care about the jewels and other stuff." De Costa did as he was told. He hoped to pocket a small handgun in the back of the safe but the stranger saw it the same time he did. "Back away from the safe." He motioned De Costa to the side of the table while he checked the money. "Wow. I feel like a genius. I'll put a little back in the safe to throw off the cops and keep the rest. Think of it like I'm giving you a speeding ticket." He laughed as they returned to the kitchen. "Boys, Mr. De Costa felt real bad about Clarence so he gave us this big stack of money. Denise, find me something to carry this in."

De Costa continued to size the men up. Reed didn't seem to pose much of a problem, looking more scared than Denise during the robbery. The man called Bobby would be more of a challenge judging from the easy way he carried himself. The tough one seemed the most dangerous so he would be the first target.

"Bobby, you'll drive my truck." He looked at the De Costas. "You two are riding with us in the back of the truck. I'll keep this gun on you every second. If you cause any trouble you're dead. Patrick you drive the old blue truck. I think I saw the keys in it."

"You said if I signed the contract you'd let us go."

The tough guy smiled.

"Your wife complicated things a little when she shot Clarence." He laughed again. "Especially for Clarence. You'll still have a chance to survive if you do what you're told. I don't think you'll run to the cops about the cash in the safe."

Enrico noticed someone had placed the shotgun he'd been cleaning on the bench of the garage in the back window of his old pick-up truck. These criminals didn't realize he always kept a box of shells in the glove box of the old truck. Payback could still be a possibility. In less than an hour he knew where they were heading. The procession of vehicles stopped on an isolated road deep into De Costa's property in the foothills. He and his wife were ordered out of the truck to face the three other men; standing alone and defenseless and blinded by the bright headlights of the monster truck. The tough guy emerged from the darkness brandishing a shotgun.

"You know, Enrico, the smart move would be to shoot you now."

"What would that get you? I signed the contract. The property is worth a lot more money than what you stole tonight. That's what you wanted, wasn't it?"

"The trouble is I'm just not sure I can trust you."

"What more can I do?"

"How do I know you're not going to run to the police if I let you go? You need to convince me you're going to hold up your end of the bargain."

"All I care about is my wife. I have plenty of money. I can afford to let the property go. I don't care what you do with it. I just want our safety."

The leader seemed to take a final moment to consider the situation.

"I hope our little episode up here will serve as a reminder to you that I can kill you or your wife any time I want." He motioned with the shotgun towards the truck. "Okay, you're free to leave."

Enrico stared at him in shock for just a second.

"Get in the truck, Denise."

Was it really possible they were going to let them go? As he was about to start the truck he got his answer.

"You know, Enrico, I just don't believe you."

Only a brief glance to his wife preceded a blinding flash of light from the shotgun.

Chapter 29

"I couldn't believe it when Monroe shot De Costa. He calmly moved the gun to his wife. She didn't even flinch. She looked him right in the eyes and took it. Then Monroe turned the gun on me. He held it there for what seemed like an eternity. I thought I was done but he seemed to change his mind. He decided to hide the truck and the bodies by pushing them into the lake.

"I realized on the way down the hill Monroe had always planned to kill Enrico. He must have decided early on he'd have a better chance of dealing with Valentino. We drove all the way down to a small dirt road south of Los Gatos. I didn't see a street sign marking it off Highway Seventeen. Monroe said it was a place where kids went to park. We drove to the very end of the road. He made me bury Waters a little ways into the brush.

"When we were done he dropped Wilson back in town then drove me to my house. He told me to keep my mouth shut or I'd be next. He said we still had a chance to pull off the real estate deal but we'd have to work it on Valentino. I didn't see how there was any chance but I wasn't in a position to argue."

When Reed finished telling the story they were both quiet for a moment. "So you're saying Wilson and Waters had been with Monroe for some time. You don't think they were recruited for this job?"

"No. Monroe and Wilson had been pulling all kinds of robberies and drug busts from the stories I heard. Waters was fairly new. He'd only been out of prison a few months."

"What happened to the gun Denise used?"

"I think Wilson threw it as far as he could into the pond when we dumped the truck."

"What happened to Wilson?"

"A couple of weeks later Monroe made me try to sell the deal to Valentino. I could tell from the first second he wasn't going to buy it so I panicked. I thought I was going to get arrested for sure after the meeting. I was surprised nothing happened right away. I started to think maybe the whole thing might blow over. I was trying to figure a way to skip town but I was afraid Monroe would come after me. He called a few days later saying it was time to split the money from the De Costa robbery so we could all lay low for a while. He picked me up and drove back to the spot where we'd buried Waters. Wilson was waiting for us beside his truck. Monroe had pulled on a pair of gloves as soon as we turned off the main road. As we pulled to a stop he left the lights on, shut off the engine and opened the door with his gun drawn. He ordered Wilson to put his hands up and told me to get his gun. As soon as I handed it to Monroe, he shot Wilson with his own gun."

"I thought it would be tricky getting rid of Wilson."

"I was scared out of my mind. Monroe walked up and kicked Wilson to make sure he was dead. He warned me if I didn't do everything he said I'd be next."

"Why'd he kill Wilson?"

"Monroe said he was always going to get rid of Wilson and his brother-in-law. They were unnecessary once the De Costas were out of the way. He wasn't going to take any chances with anyone talking."

"What did you do with Wilson's body?"

"Monroe made me bury him right beside Waters. God, the stench. I couldn't believe Waters hadn't been found."

"So the plan was always a two-way split, not four."

"It dawned on me it was always going to be a one-way split. I thought I might get it as soon as I buried Wilson but we saw another set of lights coming down the road.

"Monroe pushed me back behind his truck. He replaced his gun in his holster but kept Wilson's gun drawn. I'm sure if they'd driven all the way to the end he'd have shot them through the windshield like he did the De Costas.

"The car pulled over at a little turn-off around the curve from where we were located. I guess the kids couldn't see Monroe's truck because his lights were off. We waited a few minutes but it became obvious the car was going to be there a while. The car had us trapped with two dead bodies. Monroe ordered me to walk up to the car. He said to knock on the window and tell them to move out. While I walked up to the driver side door, Monroe worked his way around the back of the car. I started in on a story about a crime scene with the girl who was driving. She didn't seem nervous or anything and started asking questions about what was going on. Monroe quickly approached the car from the rear and stuck Wilson's pistol in the driver side window."

Reed stopped. He seemed like the whole thing was happening right in front of him all over again.

"Take your time. I've got to know everything."

"He shot the poor girl right in the face. She never knew what hit her. Her . . .brains and blood went all over the boy. He sat frozen in the seat for a second, but finally jumped out of the car and started running, but he went the wrong way. He ran back towards our truck, leaving no escape."

"Monroe killed him, too?"

"He let him run for a second and then shot him. The poor kid was writhing on the ground but Monroe was laughing like a crazy man. He motioned at me with the gun to stay with him as he approached the boy. The crotch of his jeans was covered in blood. Monroe knelt down close to his face and whispered to him for a minute."

"What'd he say?"

"I'll never forget it as long as I live. He said the kid's balls were about a hundred yards in the woods so he'd never be much of a man. He ordered him to open his mouth. He repeated it a couple of times in a soothing kind of way. Finally, the boy did what he said. Monroe put the gun in his mouth and fired.

"When he turned back to me, he pulled the other gun out of his coat. He returned to his truck and wiped off the gun he'd been using then handed it to me. He was still laughing about the boy letting him put the gun in his mouth. He found a plastic bag in the glove box and told me to drop the gun in it. He made me drag the two kids over where Wilson and Waters were but we just left them on top of the ground.

"Monroe finally took the time to explain to me I was the biggest idiot of all time. The real estate deal had always been a scheme to blame the killings on me. The real plan had always been to rob De Costa and kill him. He was a little disappointed the take was only about a hundred and fifty thousand. He'd staked out De Costa for months trying to figure out how he was going to pull it off. When he noticed me visiting the De Costa's office from time to time he started tailing me. The meeting at the Red Parrot wasn't by chance. He'd set me up from the beginning. The plan got better and better for him, though, because he could use the contract to throw the blame on me. The date on the contracts being the same as when the De Costas were killed would lead the police right back to me. Nobody would know about him. If I got arrested and tried to pin anything on him it would be my word against a cop's. He told me the smartest thing I could do was run for it. He'd shot the kids with Wilson's pistol and now he had my prints on the murder weapon. If I went to the police he could use the gun to make it look like the gang was just Wilson, Waters and me. We'd had some kind of a fight and I'd killed both of them. He had me for the two kids, too. He said we'd meet the following night at the Red Parrott so he could give me my share of the money he stole from De Costa's safe on the condition I ditched the girl's car. He'd have shot me right then if I didn't do what he said. I drove to a neighborhood that looked deserted enough for me to get away without being seen. I sat on my jacket because the seat was covered in blood. I threw it in a trash barrel as I walked to the highway. I had to hitch down seventeen to get back home. The next night when I met him at the club he only gave me three thousand dollars. He said if he ever saw me again he'd kill me. Making a run for it was an order, not a suggestion.

"I went to my office the next morning with the idea of raising more cash but the police chief from Los Gatos stopped in. I thought he was going to arrest me on the spot. I've been hiding out here ever since he let me go. I didn't know Monroe was coming after you. You've got to believe me."

"What I believe won't make any difference on what's going to happen to you. I guess Monroe was planning on taking Tanya and me to the same spot where he killed Wilson and the kids. Why didn't you turn yourself in to the police when Monroe let you go?"

"It's complicated."

"How hard could it be to drive down to the station and tell your story?"

"You don't understand. I think there's somebody else involved."

"Someone else?"

"Yes. And I think he's a cop, too."

"You're saying there were Waters, Wilson, Monroe, yourself and someone else?"

"The brains of the outfit."

"What makes you think that?"

"A few times lately Monroe would say things like let me check on it or something to that effect. He took a lot of cell phone calls, too, making me think he was taking orders. It's not like these guys were the smartest guys around. They were successful because they had protection. I think there was someone higher up running the show."

"You have any ideas?"

"No, but that's why I haven't turned myself in. I could be walking into a death trap."

McAllister considered Reed's predicament.

"So you're willing to turn yourself in but just don't know how to do it safely?"

"Exactly. Where would I go? Maybe we should drive up to San Francisco?"

"I'm not driving all the way to San Francisco with you." McAllister tried to concentrate on the quickest way to get rid of Reed. "We know we've got a dirty cop in Los Gatos and one in Monterey. I think right here in Santa Cruz would work."

"I'm still not sure I'd be safe but I know I can't run like this anymore. Would you go with me, kind of like an arresting officer?"

"I'll take you in right now. I'll guarantee you make it in one piece."

McAllister pulled out his cell phone and dialed 911.

"What are you doing?"

"It'll be simpler to let them come to us." He received a quick response to his call. "This is Michael McAllister. I'm a private investigator working on a case with the Los Gatos Police Department. I've got a wanted man with me who wants to turn himself in."

A woman's voice on the other end of the line wasn't going to make it that simple. "What's his name?"

"Patrick Reed."

The name got some very prompt service.

"Where are you?"

McAllister looked to Reed.

"What's the address?"

McAllister relayed the information and specifically requested the Santa Cruz police.

"Let me stay on the line with you. I want you to relay what I say to the cops. Ask the police officers to come to the front of the house. Have them call to me when they're ready for us to come out. I'll send Reed out first then I'll follow. I'm not taking any chances with Reed until he's in cuffs. When I see everything's okay I'll come out with my hands up."

Two cars arrived in minutes, silently but with the lights flashing. The arrest went without a hitch. The officers seemed relieved to apprehend two suspects with their hands raised. Luckily they seemed to recognize McAllister. Unfortunately, they arrested Fred, too, possibly for harboring a known criminal. He'd have to do some time until his owner returned from Europe.

McAllister was detained for an hour at the station before an officer returned him to Lucille. He snuggled up to Tanya as the neon numbers on the clock registered just past three. An offer of a super detailed report in the morning in return for sleep was readily accepted. She seemed satisfied he'd come home to her as he promised. Her mother would be another matter when the sun rose.

Chapter 30

Michael awoke in his old room at the Stafford house; feeling warm and cozy under a thick comforter. The closed curtain covering the door to the balcony had done a good job of keeping the room dark. He guessed Tanya had decided to let him sleep late as a reward for good behavior.

The cell phone sitting patiently on the night stand caught his attention. He remembered he'd turned it off at the start of his interrogation of Reed so he took a minute to check for messages. Four missed calls begged for immediate attention, one from Stacy and three from the chief. Stacy seemed the safest place to begin.

"Why didn't you call me last night? I could've helped you with Reed. How did you find him, anyway?"

"I found something at his house that led me to the other house you found on his phone records just a block away. I caught him hiding under the bed, if you can believe it. We had a nice chat and then I turned him in. It was too late to call you when I got done with the Santa Cruz police. How did you find out about it?"

"The shit has really hit the fan here. The chief is fuming about you arresting Reed without calling him."

"Don't let him know we talked yesterday. There's no sense getting your ass chewed out, too. I'll just tell him I went down to Reed's house to nose around and got lucky. I can sell it."

When her voice went up an octave, McAllister hung up and speed dialed Palatine, deciding to get chewed out right away rather than fret about it. Palatine wasn't a man to waste time. The chief didn't sound happy and McAllister wasn't in a mood to apologize. In the back of his mind McAllister had the sinking feeling the chief might fit for the fifth man. It suddenly occurred to the detective that what Reed had told him about the murders could prove deadly.

"What in the hell happened last night?"

"It's a long story."

"I've got time. I'm coming over."

"Tanya and I are at her place in San Francisco. We'll probably come down today or tomorrow. I'll call you when I get to town."

"Reed's dead you know."

One simple sentence changed everything.

"What?"

"He hung himself in his cell in Monterey last night."

"Monterey? I took him to Santa Cruz."

"Santa Cruz doesn't have a jail, dumbass. All their over-night guests get transported to Monterey. I could've told you that if you'd called me."

"I'll call you when I get to town."

McAllister hung up before the chief could reach through the phone and choke him. A shave and shower offered courage because he still had to face Tanya's mom, whom he dreaded more than any police force. A second ass chewing before lunch seemed inevitable. At eleven he headed downstairs for the penalty phase of a trial that had occurred in his absence.

Michael found Tanya with her mom seated at the kitchen table enjoying coffee. Both smiled warmly in his direction when he entered. For a moment he thought he was in the wrong house but no woman was as beautiful as Tanya. Something was up. Maybe he got the death penalty. Perhaps the pancakes were poisoned.

"Morning, honey."

Tanya jumped up and gave him a big kiss. Her mom didn't try to hit him with a hammer. When he tested them with the news about Reed they let him know they had already watched it a couple of times on television. Maybe Tanya's mom felt the case was over.

"I need to go down to Los Gatos today so I can finish this with Palatine."

Tanya continued her agreeable demeanor. "I'll drive with you. I can start getting things together at the house while you have your meeting." After a late breakfast they headed south in her car. "I had a long talk with my mom last night. We're going to take Peter's en suite. She's going to take Maria's place on the back of the house, after I remodel it of course. She doesn't want to have to climb the stairs."

"Anything you want is fine with me, princess."

"Not every man welcomes living with his mother-in-law."

"Your mother's fine. Besides, it's a big house. We might not bump into each other for weeks at a time."

"Mother also contacted a security firm. We're going to rotate two guards but they won't live in the house. A security company is scheduled to come in tomorrow to start on a new system."

McAllister envisioned a house much like an IBM office, complete with name badges, including a head shot, to get through security. At Tanya's request he cleared each room in the old Waldorf house before leaving for the station. He'd dodged one ass-chewing but doubted he'd get by another. He was right. The meeting started with a glaring contest.

"First, I want to know how you found Reed. You told me yesterday you were done with the case."

"When I came down to the station and told you I was finished with the case I still had a bad taste in my mouth so I decided to give it one last shot. I drove down to Reed's house and sifted through every piece of paper in the entire house. I figured since the cops had just been through his place they wouldn't think of someone else dropping by. I spent all day shoveling through the debris before I noticed a calendar on the wall. Three weeks were marked off for an address located close by. I walked a couple of blocks to the house and found Reed hiding under the bed."

"Why in the hell didn't you call me?"

"Reed was scared about turning himself in. He thought there was another police officer involved, the big boss."

The chief's face screwed up in deep thought and then turned an angry red. "So you decided that someone was me."

"I decided I couldn't take the chance it was you."

The revelation stopped the chief in his tracks for a few seconds.

"Why did you turn him in to Santa Cruz?"

"Monroe was from Monterey. We didn't trust them. Wilson was from Los Gatos. Reed wanted me to drive him to San Francisco but I wasn't about to sit in my small Jag all the way up there trying to keep a gun on him and drive at the same time. Santa Cruz seemed like a safe bet."

"Did you get a chance to talk to him before you turned him in?"

"I didn't call the police until he told me everything."

"I'm going to try to get past how mad I was when I found out what happened. I don't like other police departments filling me in on my own cases. I can see your point, though. I guess I might've done the same thing."

"You said Reed was dead. What happened?"

"Santa Cruz doesn't have a lock up. If someone has to be detained they call Monterey. We do the same thing. Taking him to Santa Cruz was just like taking him to Monterey; it just took him a little longer to get there. Monterey booked him late last night and this morning when the staff came around for breakfast he was swinging from the bed sheet in his cell."

"So you're saying I got him killed."

"In a round-about way, yes, but you couldn't have known."

"Do you think Reed told his story to the Santa Cruz police before he got transferred?"

"Not from what I can tell. They called their chief when he was brought in and he decided to play it safe; not wanting to risk a screw up with the interrogation. Santa Cruz just held him until Monterey came and got him. I'd say Monterey locked him up when he arrived because it was really late. Looks like you're the only one who knows what happened."

McAllister knew it was dangerous for him to be the only one to know the full story of the De Costa murders but couldn't quite figure out what to do. Others might assume he'd tell Tanya, bringing danger to both of them if there was in fact a fifth man involved in the crimes. Finally the detective came up with a plan.

"I want a witness. If you bring in Carson, I'll tell you both everything I know."

The chief didn't seem to like including Carson but McAllister insisted. McAllister related everything Reed had told him the previous night in complete detail. The chief stopped him several times to make sure he had the story straight. Almost an hour later they knew the whole story. Both winced when McAllister got to the part about the kids. Carson seemed to know the location of the road Reed described where teenagers went to park, due to some past experience that she didn't seem to want to discuss in detail. The chief ordered her to make arrangements for a search party, allowing McAllister to continue with Palatine alone.

McAllister had a final request. "I'd prefer to be the one to tell Blue what happened. After I'm done with him I really am off the case. The whole thing has turned into a big mess and I've certainly done my part to make it that way."

"What about the fifth man?"

"You figure it out. Tanya and I are moving to San Francisco as soon as possible. We're going to build a military compound at the Stafford place."

"When you talk to Blue, I'd appreciate it if you'd leave out the part about the fifth man. I have some ideas about who it might be. I want some time to work on it."

McAllister nodded in agreement and left without another word, dialing Blue just outside the station on his cell phone. De Costa had already heard about Reed on the news. McAllister promised to tell him everything if he'd come over to the old Waldorf mansion.

Chapter 31

Tanya sounded concerned when Michael invited her to sit with him by the pool. "This sounds serious. You realize, of course, breaking up isn't an option for you at this point."

Michael caught her off guard with an impromptu proposal. "Actually, I was thinking just the opposite. I think we should get married; right away if possible."

"Palatine didn't kick you in the head or anything, did he?"

He smiled and brushed her strawberry blonde hair behind her left ear. "Like you said, we got a late start. I think we need to make up for lost time."

Tanya jumped to her feet after a quick kiss for the engagement offer.

"I've got to call all my girlfriends. No, first I've got to call mother."

"Which reminds me, I invited Blue over for a drink so I can fill him in on all the details of the case. You can listen to make sure you didn't miss anything during your interrogation on the drive down this morning. There's a loose end I've got to tie up as well."

"What loose end?"

"If you haven't figured it out then you'll have to wait 'til I tell Blue. I'm a little concerned about your future as a detective."

"We're out of the detective business," she called over her shoulder as she ran inside to retrieve her cell phone.

Valentino arrived in his truck with two of his interchangeable body guards. McAllister was relieved when they stayed by the truck. He offered the trusty table by the pool with the promise of a cool drink.

When the three of them were gathered around the table De Costa began. "Please explain the case from beginning to end. I haven't been able to come up with a motive no matter how hard I've tried. I can't make sense of the facts as I know them."

McAllister took his time and walked Blue through the details Reed had told him before the police arrived, making sure De Costa understood the facts surrounding the plan to kidnap his parents and why. Blue interrupted frequently as Michael told the story. McAllister stressed it was really a robbery started by rumors of a card game where Enrico won a large sum of money. The discussion took almost an hour but Blue finally seemed satisfied. McAllister didn't mention the fifth man as he had promised the chief. Michael excused himself for a minute and retrieved the book he'd brought down from Tanya's study earlier, knowing he'd need it for the second part of their conversation.

"Blue, I want to bring to your attention this little book Tanya inherited from her uncle, Peter Stafford; the diary of Emma Waldorf. You know who she was?"

"She's the lady buried down by the racing garage, the original owner of this house."

"Yes, the mother of Jack Waldorf. May I read you some of the last few pages?"

Blue seemed confused while Tanya squirmed on the edge of her chair in anticipation. Michael opened the book to the last page and began reading.

"And a final word of advice to the youngsters from an old woman: It is my hope when you encounter a large Oak tree in the middle of the road, you will simply turn toward a flowery path. Does any of that make sense to you?"

Blue didn't hazard a guess but Tanya wasn't shy about a guess.

"It's just something about not letting obstacles deter you from your dreams, isn't it?"

"I had a talk with Buck Snider the other day. He backed up something I'd been thinking about since the first day I met you, Blue. I knew about this book so I've been checking on a few details. I think it's a clue to a mystery that's been sleeping for many years."

De Costa still seemed more confused than interested. "A clue?"

"Blue, you mentioned you'd been here before, right?"

"I told you the place seemed familiar."

"When you turned off the highway when you drove here just now, what did you find in the middle of the road?"

Tanya jumped to her feet. "The Oak tree in the middle of the road."

"Exactly. I think these clues were meant to be taken literally. You mentioned in the old days flowers lined the path to the garage. Where did the path lead?"

De Costa began to get interested. "To the grave site."

"I think we should take a little walk."

The three adjourned in the haze of the late afternoon just as the sun began to drop below the trees. Blue whispered a few orders to his guards as they left the house. They followed at a discreet distance, sensing they should not hear what was to be discussed.

As the days grew shorter the shade from the thick trees along the walk turned everything crimson brown, forming a haze but not so thick to keep them from reading the head stone when they arrived at the grave of Emma Waldorf. Michael positioned Tanya and Blue in front of the marker so they could read the writing, then continued to read again from the diary.

"It is my hope when you encounter a large Oak tree in the middle of the road, you will simply turn down a flowery path. There you will find the truth. So, we are here to seek the truth. *Remember, life can be such a simple puzzle. Count the numbers and read the words. Eight, eleven, seventeen, twenty-seven.* What do you think that means?"

Tanya guessed first. "It's a code."

She turned to inspect the inscription on the gravestone more carefully.

Emma Waldorf

1900-1981

Wife of Robert, mother of Jack,

How our lives led us down flowery

paths in mysterious ways only to

finish here by the tranquil Blue Sea.

"Tanya, count to word number eight."

"Jack."

"Eleven."

"Lives."

"Seventeen."

"In."

"Twenty-seven."

"Blue. Jack lives in Blue. What could it mean?"

"Think about it a minute. Do you remember what Peter said about Emma calling him? She demanded to be buried here with the inscription on her gravestone exactly as she said?"

"Yes, I do."

"It was a secret she felt she had to pass on, but at a time when the news wouldn't hurt anyone."

Blue grew strangely calm. "So what do you mean by all this?"

Michael looked him straight in the eye. "Jack was your grandfather."

He seemed to consider the statement then replied. "My grandfather was Mario."

"Mario pursued Christiana for some time?"

"Yes, I was told she played very hard to get."

"That was because she was in love with Jack Waldorf. She planned to marry him but he was killed in a plane crash. Buck said Christiana married very quickly after Jack was killed. Know why?"

Tanya figured it out first. "Oh my God. She was pregnant!"

Michael looked back at Blue. "Maybe she knew or maybe she found out just after Jack was killed. She married Mario quickly and tricked him into thinking the baby was his."

Blue still wasn't convinced. "Why wouldn't Enrico have had blonde hair and blue eyes if he was Jack's son?"

"The answer is basic genetics. Christiana was Italian with brown eyes and brown hair. Those traits always dominate the recessive traits of blonde hair and blue eyes."

"Then how could I have blond hair and blue eyes?

"Your mother, Denise, was an American with blonde hair and blue eyes. By the greatest coincidence you inherited the recessive genes from both your mother and father."

All stood silent for a few moments. Finally Blue spoke again. "It's an interesting theory but difficult to prove."

McAllister was ready for that response. "That's where you're wrong. Two pieces of evidence prove it beyond any doubt."

"What evidence?"

Michael opened the diary to the last page again. "The last sentence reads like this: *The truth lies in your hands as you read this passage.* What's in my hands?"

Tanya couldn't wait for Blue to figure it out. "The woven hair Emma made for a bookmark."

"When I was reading the diary yesterday, I noticed a page torn out of a magazine, folded and placed inside, an early article about DNA. I think every time Peter or Tanya might have looked at this diary, they assumed it was just a folded paper used for a bookmark. I think she found this article and realized she might be able to leave proof of Jack's ancestry. DNA was a very new and unproven concept at the end of Emma's life. It's just speculation on my part but I'd bet anything Christiana must have visited Emma at the nursing home before she died. She took you with her to let her know the truth without saying it. Emma would have felt she was looking at Jack as a child again when she saw you. I think after she found the article about DNA she cut her long hair and made a braid. With any luck she brushed her hair before she cut it. This braid could well contain mitochondrial DNA. It could certainly be tested to prove without a doubt she's related to you. I think you should take this diary with you and read it. Maybe you should consider some DNA testing."

"You said there were two pieces of evidence. What's the second?"

"Just look in the mirror, Blue. You look so identical to Jack that Buck thought he was hallucinating."

Blue slowly reached for the book and put it under his arm as he turned to walk back to the house. Tanya walked beside Michael, gripping his hand tightly. Blue turned back to face them before he reached his truck. "I remember very clearly a day long ago when Christiana brought me here as a small child. The house was abandoned so we had to move along the wall towards the creek to find a place to enter. It must have been shortly after Emma's death because the flowers were still blooming along the path. Christiana was crying. I remembered the day vividly because I'd never seen her cry before. She told me this was an important place but I had no idea what she was talking about.

"When I was in high school I learned about simple genetics in biology class. When we studied the dominant and recessive genes it seemed to me something was wrong. I came to the conclusion Enrico was not my father. I knew his heritage to the old country was unbroken. His brown eyes and dark hair would've dominated any of my mother's genes. The fact my father never once called me Blue, always Valentino, bothered me, too. I asked a few questions about how they met, how long they

191

had known each other before they got married. They must have thought it was cute at the time. I came to the conclusion my father must have known the truth but I never had the courage to ask him about it. I guess I was scared to really know so I finally let it go. I decided if my father was okay with it then I should be as well. I convinced myself Enrico was not my biological father. Somehow it never dawned on me to go back one more generation.

"Seeing the mural on the back wall of the garage was a jolt. I guess eventually I might've arrived at the same conclusion as you." De Costa turned toward the truck, then stopped and turned back to face Michael. "There's a much simpler way to get to the bottom of this. I'll just ask Christiana."

Michael had never considered the fact that Christiana might still be alive.

"Mario died years ago but Christiana is still in pretty good health. She's always been very close to me. I think I remember catching her reading about you and Tanya renovating this place in the paper one day. She nearly jumped out of her skin when I asked her about it. I certainly don't want to hurt her but since you've allowed me to borrow Emma's diary I can use it as an excuse to bring this whole thing to a conclusion. I'll pretend ignorance and ask her to explain the words at the end of the diary. She'll tell me the truth."

De Costa nodded to his guards and they left. Michael wondered what thoughts were going through Blue's mind as he slowly drove away from the estate. Tanya put her arm through his as they walked to the back of the house. Michael reclaimed his lounge chair by the pool while she refreshed their drinks, a glass of Syrah for her, Diet Dr. Pepper for him.

"When did you know?"

"The first time we visited Buck in Santa Cruz he mentioned seeing Jack when he was in town from time to time."

"Yes, I remember the conversation."

"Well, Buck didn't seem like he was crazy to me. I thought it was the strangest thing I'd ever heard. When Blue came to the racing garage, I knew he was the person Buck had seen in town. The resemblance was too close to be by chance. I just didn't have time until now to figure it out."

"Boy, when you take a case, you really follow it to the end."

"It's what detectives do, princess. They detect."

Chapter 32

Michael and Tanya slowly built a new lifestyle in San Francisco over the next month. Derek Hunter was hired to move the cars back to the under-ground garage at the Stafford place. A professional cleaned and waxed the Jags to complete the display as it was the first time McAllister saw it in the underground garage. Tanya seemed have lost interest in contesting the racing series for the next year. No calls came from Palatine or De Costa. The papers didn't report anything about the arrest of a fifth man in the De Costa case and the whole series of events began to fade.

The renovation of the rooms for her mother required Tanya's full focus but Michael struggled with boredom. Nothing went unnoticed by his girl and she came up with a solution.

"Jay Leno offered to let you come visit his garage for a story about his Jags. You should give him a call. His collection would make a great column."

Michael had met Jay Leno at several Pebble Beach functions over the last two years. Leno had seen Lucille and learned about her heritage at the special exhibit at Pebble Beach. He'd readily offered a visit to Burbank to see his collection. Michael was surprised on his initial phone call to learn Leno owned several Jaguars, an easy tie-in for a story. Jay left the details to be worked out with his assistant at the television station. The Jay Leno name had a magical effect on people. Michael had done quite a number of interviews by this time; many of them well-known classic car collectors, but no one in the car business had Leno's star power. If Michael could write a compelling story with some good pictures of the garage it would elevate his status a notch in the writing business.

Performing an in-depth interview presented a challenge. The first day after they became a couple, Tanya told Michael she was going to sleep with him every night for the rest of their lives; a rule she took seriously. Tanya's schedule was adjustable to a point but not for days at a time. Jay wanted Michael to drive down in Lucille. Tanya remained adamant it would have to be a one day trip.

"You'll have to figure out a way to get this done and still be home by nightfall. You'll probably have to get up about four in the morning to drive down to Los Angeles. You can make it in five hours if you really hustle. Take as long as you want with the interview and pictures but just know you are going to drive back in the evening. I don't care what time it is when you get home but you're sleeping with me."

Tanya could be persuasive when she put her mind to it. She'd agreed to spend a couple of nights in Los Gatos, saving Michael two hours driving time each way, because she could use the time to box up some of the last remaining items for the move north. The Waldorf mansion was to be sold largely furnished. Jay agreed on the following Tuesday as the date for the interview.

McAllister had orders to arrive by ten if possible because Leno had to be at the studio no later than noon.

Tanya worked out a good set of directions on her computer, a trip of a little over three hundred miles each way. Great time would be five hours even. Tanya wasn't kidding when she said he'd have to be up and on the road by four. Michael spent some time on the computer himself during the next two days as he prepared thoroughly for his interview. Jay had a well-designed web site describing various cars in his garage, providing a great amount of detailed information. The story needed a focus. Michael zeroed in on three Jags, a highly customized E-type and two XK120s, in the collection.

The alarm on his cell phone proved sufficiently annoying to get him out of bed when the day of the trip arrived. Michael stumbled into the shower while Tanya made a bold attempt to ignore the disturbance, but she got up when he started dressing; preparing a breakfast as well as a small cooler stuffed with energy bars and Diet Dr. Peppers.

"You know I'd pay you considerably more than the magazine to hang around with me all the time."

"You made it quite clear the last time I went to work with you that one day projects took three days when I went along to help."

She considered his comment and seemed to remember why she had suggested the trip. Arm in arm they walked out to Lucille in the darkness. The morning air was cool but dead calm. He hugged her for a minute while Lucille warmed up. Tanya gave strict instructions to call on his way back, so she would know when to expect him.

McAllister was a little surprised at the quickest route south. He thought he'd be taking the 101 but it turned out cutting through the mountains to Highway 5 would save a lot of time. The winding road challenged Lucille until they dropped out of the hills to the highway. An endless ribbon of pavement split the San Joaquin Valley down the middle. Tumbleweeds seemed to be the valley's main product. As the sun rose miles of ranchland appeared, peppered with cattle trying to figure out why anyone would put them in a place with so little grass. Occasionally his nose told him he'd passed a slaughterhouse; the last round-up for the condemned. Tanya had suggested they become vegetarians and the idea gained merit.

A big truck station near the Bakersfield exit provided a break after more than two hours. After filling the Jag he used the facilities and took a few minutes to stretch his back and legs. Lucille's speedometer needle had remained buried above eighty during the long, boring drive. At the south end of the San Joaquin valley Lucille had to work hard for a half hour to climb through a pass. Two hours after they started descending the other side they arrived at the gate to Leno's garage in Burbank. A short session with an intercom caused the gate to flinch and then roll to one side. A rather distinguished gentleman came out of a door across the lot as he pulled into a parking space.

"My name is Bernard. I'm the chief mechanic and engineer. Jay is running late. He asked me to show you around. Did you know I used to own a Jaguar restoration shop in Los Gatos?"

The information caught McAllister by surprise. "I think I actually went to your shop recently. I heard you retired."

"My plan changed when Jay made me an offer I couldn't refuse. I've built a lot of Jags in my day. I like your one-fifty; Lucille I think you call her. I was with Jay at Pebble Beach when the Waldorf Jags were on display."

Bernard ignored McAllister while he inspected the vintage beauty but later insisted McAllister raise the hood so he could have a look at the engine compartment. A blast of hot air caught Michael by surprise, the result of a morning of hard work.

"Follow me inside and we'll get coffee."

They entered the door to what seemed to be the main building, actually a converted aircraft hangar. Burbank Airport was adjacent to the site but the main terminal was on the other side of the runways. An immense room emerged containing what seemed like ten or twelve bays for projects, all of them occupied. McAllister observed four technicians working on various cars. The walls were covered with monstrous automobile signs of Duesenberg and other classic brands; truly a car guy's paradise. Bernard directed him to a large granite covered table.

"Can I get you a coffee or cappuccino?"

McAllister spied a soft drink machine against the wall. "I think I'll just get a diet drink if that's okay." He fumbled in his pockets for change, causing Bernard to laugh.

"You don't need money for the machines here. Jay takes good care of us. Just pull what you want."

Once armed with their drinks they began a tour of the other buildings, five in total covering approximately 100,000 square feet. The structures contained more than 130 cars and possibly the same number of motorcycles. The Jaguars Michael had researched were on display in the farthest corner of the last building. Bernard continued in his role as tour guide.

"The E-type is an interesting car. There's not another like it in the world. We customized a series three car by cutting about six inches out of the middle and then welded in covered headlights to make it look like a series one. The V-twelve motor makes it fast and the shorter wheelbase makes it agile."

After furiously writing notes and then shooting seventy-five pictures Michael turned to the XK120s, one white and the other blue. As Bernard prepared to give Michael the information on the two classics, Jay called out from across the room.

"Sorry I'm late, Michael. I got held up working on the monologue for today's show. Where are we?"

"We were just starting on the one-twenties."

"Okay. Notice the enlargement of the poster on the wall? That's a poster used when these cars came out in the early fifties. I decided to duplicate the sign with two cars, one a roadster and the other a fixed head. The white car is highly modified to go fast so under the hood it's not stock. The original motor is displayed by the wall." He quickly motioned behind them towards a stand and motor; cam covers shining with a mirror finish. "The blue car I bought just as it is, a near perfectly restored car.

"There's an interesting story that goes with the blue Jag. I found it in San Diego. After arranging the purchase I decided to fly down and drive it home myself. The owner picked me up at the airport, we completed the transaction and soon I was cruising out of the neighborhood in my new car. After only a few blocks I passed by a golf course and guess what? An errant ball flew over the fence and hit the car in the front by the headlight. We still haven't gotten around to fixing the dent."

He pointed out a perfect half golf ball impression just below the headlight. It seemed refreshing to know things like that even happened to Jay Leno. His host accompanied McAllister on the remainder of the tour. Michael was allowed to shoot pictures of the other cars, not for the article, but as a private memory of the day.

"Want to see the treasure room?" Of course Michael nodded in the affirmative.

Jay led the way back to the main building and walked to the far side of the room from the main entrance. Michael hadn't noticed the small door earlier, which led to a special room. Inside a line of Duesenbergs on one wall faced a similar line of Bugattis on the other. One car resplendent in French blue immediately caught Michael's attention. Leno explained the car was a recreation of a Bugatti Atlantic. Michael had never heard of the car before, but it was the most beautiful piece of rolling artwork he'd ever seen; even sporting a riveted fin running down the middle of the body.

"Only three of them exist so I most likely won't get a chance to buy one. We bought an authentic chassis and motor and Bernard supervised construction of a body made from aluminum. Some people think a fourth one exists but I doubt it will ever show up. Someone would have found it by now if it was still around."

Jay apologized and disappeared a few minutes later. What had seemed like thirty minutes turned out to be well over two hours. Bernard made sure Michael bagged a sandwich for the trip home then walked him back out to Lucille and gave her the once over again while Michael packed his notebook and camera for the trip home, waving goodbye as Lucille eased out the gate. Some serious work back home could produce his best column since the Pebble Beach stories from a year before. Michael pulled to the side of the road a block outside the gate and dutifully called Tanya on her cell.

"How was it?"

"Car-guy heaven. I recorded loads of pictures and plenty of information for my story. Jay was quite cordial and offered a lot of insight on the cars."

"I got bored in Los Gatos so I organized the best lunch of all time back in San Francisco with my girlfriends. We're making big plans. The wedding is going to cost you plenty."

"Should I rob a bank on the way home?"

"Just hit the road, Jag-boy. You can beat the traffic if you hustle. You should be home around seven. You're doing well. I'm getting a little horny so you better conserve your energy."

Tanya's incentive encouraged McAllister push down hard on the accelerator. The same station near Bakersfield served as a pit stop a little over two hours later. The sky was beginning to darken as he exited the main highway for the trip across the mountains on the final leg to Los Gatos. When he dialed Tanya's cell phone for a progress report, he was surprised to hear Chief Palatine's voice.

"What are you doing with Tanya's phone?"

"Where are you?"

"I'm about an hour away. Where's Tanya?"

"Get home as fast as you can. If the police stop you tell them you're working for me."

McAllister tried to get more information but the chief hung up on him. Michael hit the redial but Palatine wouldn't pick up. A million thoughts ran through his mind. The worst one involved a recurring theme that Palatine might be the fifth man. Had the chief done something to Tanya? McAllister made Lucille work a lot harder than she might have preferred on the final leg of the trip but she didn't complain.

Chapter 33

Michael could see blue lights blazing against a dark sky a half mile from the exit to the mansion. Three police cars blocked the middle of the road when he turned onto the side road, blocking him from the gate entrance. Abandoning Lucille at the side of the road, he sprinted past the road block. As he passed the first line of police cars he could see a car wrapped around the giant oak tree in the middle of the road. A few strides later he realized it was Tanya's Jaguar. Palatine turned and saw him at the same instant. The chief caught him with a bear hug in full stride before he could reach the wreck.

"She's not in the car."

"Is she okay? What happened?"

"Get your car and follow me to the house. We need to talk."

"Is she alive? You've got to tell me."

"We don't know. Just do as I said, okay? I'll explain everything."

Michael hustled back to retrieve Lucille. A couple of officers guided him through the obstructions. He slowed as he passed the wreck carefully observing the wreckage of Tanya's once beautiful Jag. It looked as though it had been rammed in the side, right where Tanya would have been sitting in the driver's seat. Where was the other car? Had it already been removed? He sped up the drive and left his Jag by the house, screaming as he ran to the Palatine's SUV.

"What's going on?"

"She's been kidnapped."

"Kidnapped?" In a strange way the word provided relief. At least she might still be alive. "How do you know?"

"Let's talk inside." McAllister quickly unlocked the door to allow Palatine and a couple of his officers inside. The chief finally offered an explanation. "Several of the neighbors heard a crash around five. It must have been a pretty big bang because these houses are not exactly close together. A gentleman a couple of houses away came to investigate and caught a glimpse of a big truck speeding away. He couldn't identify it by make but it was one of those huge jobs with over-sized tires. Tanya was already missing from the Jag so I assume whoever was driving grabbed her. Your neighbor immediately phoned the police on his cell. One of my men got here in less than ten minutes. The officer recognized the address and especially Tanya's car because he'd seen her driving it. The driver's side window was broken out." He looked McAllister directly in the eye. "You might as well know we found blood spatter both inside and outside the car. We sealed off the scene a few minutes later. When we got reinforcements we started investigating. An envelope had been placed on Tanya's seat after the wreck."

"How do you know it was after the wreck?"

"The envelope was clean even though the seat was bloody. It must have been carefully placed there. The note read something like, 'I've left ample evidence as to who I am. I've taken Tanya. In two days you will receive my demands.' That's how we know she's been kidnapped."

"Michael turned to the other officers and motioned them outside. "This has something to do with the De Costa case. It's the fifth man."

"I can't prove it, yet, but I don't think so. We'll take her car downtown and go over every inch of it. If there's a fingerprint anywhere, we'll find it."

Just as he finished one of Palatine's men burst in.

"We found the truck. It's only a few miles away."

Palatine wrinkled his forehead at McAllister. "You want to ride with me?"

The second crime scene emerged at the end of a ten minute scramble at high speed with sirens blaring and lights flashing. A police unit with its lights flashing protected a huge truck parked at the curb of a quiet street in a rural area. The patrolman volunteered a quick assessment as soon as Palatine, with McAllister as a shadow, arrived.

"An old lady across the street saw the truck drive up and park. She was mad because another car had been parked in front of her house all day. The driver of the truck was in a hurry because the brakes squealed when it arrived. A man got out, opened the trunk of the first car, walked to the rider's side door, took something out and put it in the trunk. The something was big because it was difficult for him to get it over his shoulder."

"Did she happen to get a description of the car?"

"She did better than that. She took a picture of it with her cell phone. Can you believe it? She must be eighty. She whipped out her cell phone and took several pictures of the car including the tag number. We're running the plates. With a little luck we could catch him while he's still driving his getaway car."

The chief borrowed a flashlight for a quick look at the truck.

"I can see plenty of blood on the rider's side seat and window. I want this truck hauled downtown and put inside for the night. We'll check it over tomorrow morning. Until then nobody touches anything."

The chief said something McAllister didn't want to think about on the ride back. "With your experience, you know what we're dealing with here. You better hope against hope we get some kind of a break in the next few days." He looked him right in the eye again for a moment as he drove. "These things don't usually end well. I'll do everything humanly possible to help but the odds are against us. You better prepare yourself for the worst. Where in the hell were you?"

"Down in LA doing an interview with Jay Leno. I left early this morning so I could get down and back in a day."

"When was the last time you spoke with Tanya?"

"Right after lunch."

"Everything seemed okay?"

"Yes. She had lunch with some friends in San Francisco. We'd decided to get married. She must have been making plans with her friends."

"You'll be the one they contact. Be sure and keep your cell phone charged and with you every minute. You'll get a call or a text with instructions. Tanya will tell them or him or whoever how to contact you. I'm going to keep an officer with you twenty-four hours a day. We'll be able to mobilize in minutes when you're notified." He paused for a second then continued. "I've got to bring in the FBI. We've got the car and license. The larger the network of agencies we have looking for the car, the better our chances of getting lucky. I know they'll take control but I think it's our best bet."

When they returned home Tanya's car was being hauled away on the back of a flatbed truck. When the chief dropped him off Michael knew there was one more thing he had to do. A cell phone call had never taken so much courage.

"Mom, its Michael. Is anyone there with you?"

"My staff is here. Why?"

"Sit down. I've got some bad news."

"Something's happened to Tanya?"

"She's been kidnapped."

"Kidnapped? That's impossible. I was just with her a few hours ago."

"When I got back from Los Angeles I found her car smashed into the tree in front of the house with police swarming the scene. She was gone but he left a note. He, and I say he because the letter used the term I, he said he would be in touch with his demands in two days."

A long silence on the other end of the phone preceded words from a woman with the knowledge of a thousand years and Fort Knox at her disposal. "If this has something to do with the De Costa case, I'll never forgive you." She paused to let the threat soak in a little. "Keep me informed any developments." McAllister winced at the sound of the phone on the other end of the line slamming into its receiver.

Chapter 34

Tanya dreamed she was in the middle of a tornado, the wind blowing mercilessly, throwing houses and cars around like toys. Suddenly her father appeared. She grabbed his arm but the wind was too strong. His hand slipped from her grasp and disappeared into the darkness.

Awaking briefly and bathed in complete and utter darkness, she felt her hands and feet bound. Lying on her back she raised her arms but bumped against a low metallic wall. The grinding of an engine provided a sensation like riding in a casket at a hundred miles an hour. She lapsed back into unconsciousness before she could make sense of the situation.

Awaking a second time, she seemed to be lying on her back but now on a bed, still bound hand and foot, a prisoner in a dark cell except for a tiny window at least a thousand feet away and covered by bars. What crime had she committed? Again she passed out before she could come up with an answer.

The next time she awoke the room was light. Slowly a ceiling came into focus. Large redwood beams crossed every two feet or so. Raising her hands in front of her face she was relieved to find them unbound. A close inspection showed red skin and a residue of glue around both wrists, possibly the result of having been bound with duct tape. A quick twitch of her feet revealed them to be free as well. When she attempted to swing her feet over the side of the bed so she could sit up, bolts of lightning flew through her sides, arms and legs like electrical shocks. A second, more gingerly approach was successful. What she thought was a bed turned out to be a mattress lying flat on the floor. As she sat up the room started spinning slowly. A dull throbbing in her head made her think she had been drugged.

Bracing her aching back against the wall, she reconstructed the previous day. When she was almost home from her trip to San Francisco, a large truck had appeared from nowhere, following closely. The road was winding so she decided the other driver just wanted to get by. Less than a mile from her turn, she was sure the truck would go on when she reached her street. When she took the corner the truck slowed then followed. She pulled in front of the big oak tree in the middle of the road, instead of going around it as usual. She decided as she hit the button to open the gate if the truck stopped she wouldn't enter the grounds because no one was home to help her in case of trouble. Knowing better than to allow herself to be trapped alone, she felt she had a better chance of escaping outside the grounds. As the gate opened the truck sped up, shining its bright lights and bearing directly down on her. When it became clear he was going to ram she quickly unfastened her seatbelt and lunged to the other side of the car, probably saving her life in the process. The impact was the last thing she remembered.

A feeling of panic started to set in until she thought of Michael. He had acted so calmly when Monroe pointed a gun at them. She realized her survival depended on keeping a clear head. Begin by collecting every piece of information from the surroundings. Years of designing provided a lot of knowledge about how rooms were constructed. If it had been a normal room she could have kicked in the sheetrock and escaped between the studs, but this was no normal room. The walls were constructed solely of cinder block but with an eerily familiar odor, not musty like an old house but instead like new construction. The cinder blocks must have been laid recently, explaining the pungent scent of mortar still in the air.

The prison cell, that was the only way to describe it, did seem to be part of a house, or more correctly, the basement of a house. The wall with the window was cement and part of the foundation of the house. The other three walls had been covered with the cinder block to make an effective jail. The ceiling was high, at least ten feet, maybe eleven. A light was centered on the ceiling but no switch was available on the wall, possibly covered by the blocks. An examination of the three cinder walls did not reveal a single weakness she could exploit. Oddly, the door was indented about six inches and appeared to open outwards into the hall. The hinges were hidden safely on the other side so there was no way to attack them. The only feature on the door was a large metal slot, possibly for delivering food. She noted it could also be used to observe her unless she crouched in a corner. The only piece of furniture in the room was a small side table with a single drawer. All these things were observed while she sat with her back against the wall. Finally, she painfully pulled herself up to investigate the table. A glass of water and a sandwich in a plastic bag rested on a paper plate with a message written on it.

"Tanya: I suggest you eat the sandwich and drink the water to stay healthy. You can pee in the glass after you drink the water. This will be your only sustenance till this evening. I will be back after my errands to introduce myself. You will have all day to escape but you have a decision to make. If escape is impossible, it would be better to conserve your energy."

The note was signed with just the capital letter 'C' written in a fancy script.

"You're damn right I'm going to try to escape." She said out loud to no one in particular.

The window was the last item to be investigated as a possible escape route. High on the wall and fairly small, she stood below it and extended her arms, still a good three feet from the bottom. Moving closer she could see it was covered with a set of burglar bars, mounted into the frame of the window and curving into the room about three inches. She tested the distance with a jump but was far short of being able to reach the bottom bars. She moved to the far side of the room to observe the window more carefully. At about eighteen inches high and possibly two feet across, she could easily escape if she could somehow remove the bars. Moving the sandwich and water glass to the floor, she dragged the table under the window. She estimated she would still not quite be able to touch the bottom rungs of the bars even standing on the small table but she was sure she could jump and catch them. Walking around the room for a few minutes to loosen up, her body still felt stiff and sore. Painfully she first moved to the top of the table, and then rested her hand against the wall for balance as she stood. Looking up at the bars she gauged exactly how she wanted to catch them. On her first jump she managed to grab a bar with her right hand but missed with the left, twisting away from the wall and losing her grip. The table dealt a glancing blow as she crashed down and careened across the room, severely twisting her ankle as she hit the floor. She curled into a fetal position, hugging her legs to her chest as the pain shot to her head. After a minute she climbed back on the table to try again. Catching the bar again with one hand, this time she managed to twist around and grasp another bar with her other hand. With a burst of energy she pulled herself up so she could see outside. The sun shone brightly on a manicured lawn at eye level. Working her hands up a few inches while bracing her knees against the wall she managed a view to the outside. A large park or grounds began on the other side of the street but in the distance a beautiful building shone sharply in the late daylight, one she instantly recognized.

The Santa Barbara Mission stood in plain view, recognizable to her because of her studies while attending UCSB. Research papers on the mission style were standard college fare because of their influence on California design but this was the only one in the state with two bell towers. Parking in front of the very house that now held her prisoner was a common practice when visiting the facility because the building was surrounded on the other three sides by woods. Her captor could not have possibly known her background or the window would have been covered. The question now was how could she use this piece of information to her advantage?

The window was covered in a thick piece of Plexiglas screwed tightly into the frame inside the bars, fitting perfectly flush with the cement wall. After studying it carefully she dropped back down to the table.

Absent mindedly picking up the water and sandwich, she sat back on the mattress and ate as she ran scenarios through her mind, dismissing one after another. Although encouraged to know her location, she worried because she was a long way from Michael and any help he could bring. As she leaned against the cold cinder block wall, salt from her sweat dripped into several bleeding scrapes on her back and arms causing them to sting. Escape seemed impossible.

Chapter 35

McAllister slept fitfully in fifteen minute spurts with one hour ceiling staring spells interspersed. At four he gave up. After a shower he bumped into an officer downstairs who had just made fresh coffee. McAllister stuck to his usual drink.

"What time does Palatine get to the office?"

"Nine, like clockwork, but he'll be early for sure today."

"Why do you say that?"

"Carson came in last night to process the Jaguar and the truck to see if she could find any evidence. I'm sure she pulled an all-nighter. The chief will want to know if anything turned up."

McAllister's cell phone suddenly rang, sending an electric shock through his body. Thoughts of the kidnapper faded when the call display identified the chief.

"Come down to my office at ten so I can catch you up on what we know."

McAllister parked Lucille outside the station ten minutes early, waiting by the car and staring at his watch for an excruciating nine minutes. Palatine's assistant waved him directly into the chief's office as soon as he entered the waiting area.

"Don't sit down. We're heading to the evidence building."

In three minutes they arrived at a building containing Tanya's Jag and the truck, both recovered during the night. A very dirty and tired looking Stacy Carson offered a brave smile. McAllister let the chief handle things.

"Anything, yet?"

"I'm sure we've got something on the envelope. I think he licked it when he sealed it because it tested positive for DNA. Of course it'll take weeks to get the results."

"We don't have weeks. What else have you got?"

"I went over the truck for hours. He must've been wearing gloves every time he used it because I can't find a print anywhere. I'm checking Tanya's car now but it's covered in prints, almost too many. It'll take quite a while to process all of them. I wouldn't count too much on a match, not with the care he took on the truck."

"Try to find a stopping place and go home so you can rest. Get back on the Jag as soon as you feel up to it." The chief turned to McAllister. "Have you eaten anything lately?" McAllister offered a shrug. The chief decided he meant to say no. "I'm taking you to an early lunch or late breakfast, whatever you want to call it."

The chief drove to a pancake place downtown where they could watch the news on the big screen television while they ate. McAllister bravely pushed his food around on the plate for a few minutes before giving up. An old man bumped into him, spilling coffee on his shirt, adding insult to injury. Nothing seemed to be going his way. The old man apologized but McAllister had to accept the fact he'd be wearing a big brown splotch on his shirt all day.

"Chief, tell me you've found something."

"We installed six photo cameras on the busiest intersections in town over the past twelve months with funds from a federal grant. I'm sure we got our boy when he left your house to dump the truck. I think we'll get him after he left in the car, too. We've got every cop in the state looking for the car. We caught a huge break getting the tag number."

As they ate a bulletin came on the local news showing a picture of a car like the one that had been parked as a get-away car with the license number. Within ten minutes Palatine's phone rang.

"Yes. Yes. Okay, we'll be right there. Lester put this on the city tab. We've got to run." The chief filled McAllister in as he drove. "A guy called the station who said he rented a garage to someone who had a car like the one on television. It's only a few minutes away."

When they arrived an older gentleman was waiting for them outside an industrial looking two-story building. Unlocking a four car garage he pointed out a small office in the corner and said a loft was located at the top of the stairs. The missing car sat serenely in the middle of the space.

The chief immediately turned to McAllister. "Do you have a gun?"

218

"Just my back-up. You took the other one as evidence on the Monroe shooting."

Palatine hurried back to his truck and retrieved a shotgun from the back. McAllister could hear him calling for back-up as he ran.

"Know how to use this?" McAllister nodded. "We're not waiting. Follow me. I'm going upstairs." He motioned to the owner to move outside.

The chief ascended the stairs like a giant bull with McAllister covering the rear. A sparsely furnished and antiseptically clean bedroom was revealed when he switched on the light. A small kitchenette offered an opportunity to prepare simple meals but not a single glass or plate was in sight. With little doubt the room had been cleaned of evidence, they trudged back downstairs to ask the owner a few more questions.

"When did your tenant rent this building?"

"Almost six months ago. His lease is up in a few weeks. So far he hasn't seemed like he wanted to renew."

"We'll need the contract for evidence."

"No contract. I mean he refused to sign one. He paid me cash. I needed the money so I took it."

"What was his name?"

"No name."

"You rented to an unknown person?"

"Like I said, I needed the money and he paid cash. I didn't see how I could lose on a deal like that."

"Have you been in contact with him?"

"I live just across the street so I've seen him occasionally. He was friendly enough. He said I could check the place whenever I wanted."

"What did he say he was using it for?"

"He said he fixed up old cars and trucks to resell. He seemed pretty handy. He had three cars and a truck in here last week."

"Was it a real big black truck?"

"That's the one."

"What about the other cars?"

"He drove this one most of the time. I never saw the other two because they were always covered. He said they were parts cars."

"Okay. First, this is a crime scene. The car and the truck were used in a kidnapping. We're going to have to close this place off and check it thoroughly for evidence. Do me a favor, though." The man nodded. "I don't want you to tell anyone about this for the time being. I don't want to broadcast we found this place. There's a small chance he might come back. If you see him, call me immediately. Whatever you do, don't approach him. He's extremely dangerous."

"One more thing." The chief nodded for him to continue. "This isn't the way the place was when I rented it to him."

"What do you mean?"

"Well, the place was a lot dirtier than this. He painted everything white since the last time I was in here. The walls used to be blue. The floor was stained. Now everything is spotless."

The man hustled up the stairs to check the bedroom.

"Same up here. This is much cleaner than when I rented it to him."

New paint didn't give them much hope of finding any evidence. When he had the building secured Palatine drove McAllister back to Lucille at the station.

"I had a long chat with the FBI last night. They'll be taking control later today. We'll get the DNA results back a lot quicker with their help. I'll keep the building under surveillance until they take over but I don't think he'll be back. I think he had two more cars to use after he took Tanya but for now we have no idea what those cars look like. Go back to your place and wait for the call. The FBI will be over soon enough."

McAllister spoke half under his breath. "He's been planning this for a long time."

The chief nodded. Defeat showed on his face as he pulled into the parking lot at the station, an attitude that didn't exactly build McAllister's confidence. The detective was encouraged they would have help from the FBI. He wanted all the help they could get.

Chapter 36

The room gradually darkened as day one of her captivity drew to a close, causing Tanya to shiver slightly. Sitting on the mattress with her back to the wall, she pulled a solitary blanket around her shoulders for warmth. The room had refused to give up any secrets. Oddly a strong smell of ham suddenly permeated the darkness. The slot in the door banged open with a loud clang causing Tanya to flinch, amplified by a day of complete silence. A sinister whisper followed.

"Lay on your back on the mattress with your arms at your side. Do this immediately. If you try anything I will shoot you without hesitation."

When she complied a strong mechanical noise signaled the bolt moving inside the lock. A sinister figure entered the room carefully. By this time Tanya's eyes were well adjusted to the darkness. Surprisingly her captor appeared to be an older man, slightly bent at the waist, walking with a serious limp in his right leg, noticeable with his first few steps. He didn't appear to bother with a disguise or attempt to mask his appearance in any way. As he drew closer the smell of ham was joined by a putrid human odor. Her captor didn't seem to care much about hygiene. Before he spoke he made a slow, careful assessment of the room.

"Did you spend much time trying to escape today?" Tanya refused to answer. He ignored her small gesture of defiance. "I hope not because I can assure you, I went to great lengths to make sure escape would be impossible. I applaud any attempts but they will be hopeless." He turned to address her directly. "Hopeless is probably a key word for you now. You will live or die, suffer or prosper, strictly on my whims. Do you have anything at all to say for yourself?"

"If you want money, I can afford to pay you very well if you let me go."

"Do I appear to need money? Perhaps I should pay more attention to my appearance? I must be projecting a poor image. I'm afraid I have plenty of money and I can get more any time I want easily enough.

"I brought you something to eat. I'll leave it on the table. You may eat when I leave. I see you ate your first meal. I can tell by the aroma you also peed in the glass as I ordered."

"I need to use the bathroom, a real bathroom."

"I'll consider your request. Think about what you can offer me in return. I'm going upstairs for a few minutes. I expect you to be finished with your food and drink when I return. I'll discard anything you haven't consumed."

He left with the paper cup and package from the earlier meal. Tanya realized she had to stay nourished to have any chance for survival. A foot-long sub-style hot ham and cheese sandwich had been provided with a large soft drink. She wasted no time gulping both down.

She'd prepared for this first encounter with her captor, planning to observe him carefully. Would it be possible for her to overpower this older man? Possibly. The fact that he was alone appeared to be another break in her favor. His ability to enter the house without being detected was troubling. In spite of the fact she'd been in utter silence the entire day she hadn't heard him open or shut any doors. How could he have managed a set of very ancient stairs so quietly? She'd studied the architecture of the homes in this very neighborhood. The city of Santa Barbara allowed very little in the way of new construction, especially in the area around the mission. The ancient wood floors and stairs creaked under the slightest weight and yet he moved about undetected. Her sobering conclusion was that he was very skilled at breaking and entering; a highly talented criminal.

A few minutes later the slot opened again. He jerked it hard for effect again to scare her. Remembering an off-hand remark from Michael about his cases she knew showing fear could trigger even worse behavior from her captor. Staying calm seemed her best defense.

"I've considered your request. If I let you use the bathroom just down the hall, what will you give me in return?"

"I don't have anything to give you."

"I disagree. You're quite an attractive woman, Tanya. May I call you Tanya? What can you offer me?"

"If you try to rape me I'll fight you."

"Unfortunately for me, at my age and condition, sex is not an option. I can assure you in my youth I would have raped you repeatedly by now. No, I think maybe just a little show will have to do, a little titillation if you will. Why don't you strip? I'll allow you to use the bathroom down the hall for two minutes if you strip naked for me. What's your answer?"

Tanya's mind was racing. She decided to test him to gauge if there was any chance to manipulate him.

"I won't strip naked for you. I'll strip to my bra and panties. That's all you're going to get."

"What if I say you're going to strip naked or I'll kill you where you stand?"

After a moment of consideration to find just the right response she stood her ground. "I'd say you'd gone to a lot of trouble for nothing."

A brief silence made her wonder if she'd gone too far.

"I'm impressed. You're capable of a thought process. Okay, I agree. Strip to your underwear. I'll watch of course."

The small humiliating victory made her realize she didn't have to submit to everything he asked. On the contrary, he didn't seem like he wanted her to. Unfortunately she was wearing a thin sports bra and a thong bikini, making her close to naked when her jeans and blouse lay on the floor.

"I'll back out the door. Do not get within six feet of me at any time. Turn to your right down the hall. The bathroom is the first door on your left. Remember, two minutes."

She memorized the walls and ceiling of what appeared to be a fairly small house, the basement wall on the back of the house visible as she entered the hallway. Running her hand along the wall to her left she felt the door about ten feet down the hall. A small filthy toilet was just visible in the corner which she needed to use urgently.

"Don't close the door. I'm going to watch you."

She shut the door firmly, feeling the handle as she did so to see if it had a lock of some kind but not able to tell for sure. As she sat on the toilet she noted it was a very small but normal bathroom with traditional walls, not cinder block; a room that offered a chance to escape. Finishing quickly she counted another small victory by closing the door in his face but she didn't want to push her luck. She turned her back as he watched her dress back in her cell. Ignoring the risk she pushed for more information.

"How did you manage to find a house with its own prison cell? Surely there aren't many on the market these days."

"I built your cell, as you call it, myself. I had to be sure it was constructed properly for what I had in mind."

"You built a prison cell in the basement of your house?"

"This isn't my house. The owners are off in Europe for six months. I decided to borrow it. I think they'll be surprised when they get back. I hope they like what I've done."

"You built a prison cell in a friends' house?"

"You should know a man like me doesn't have friends. I like the fact that you're trying to collect information. I find it amusing. Usually I must endure a lot of crying and screaming."

"You've done this before?"

His answer was chilling. "I've been doing this for well over forty years. Now, pretend you're me. The challenge was to find a house that would be vacant for six months or so. I simply went to a local travel agent and said I was planning a six month trip to Europe. She seemed very excited. After she worked out a plan costing many thousands of dollars I asked her for references. She said three local couples used her for trips every year. I simply checked each house to find the one most suitable."

"You checked the houses?"

"Yes, of course. I always do so in advance. I entered in the night, when the owners were asleep, and went through their records. I found these tenants were leaving at the right time. The basement was ideal, although I did have to install the cinder block. It took a week of pretty difficult work."

"How did you manage to get the cinder blocks into the house without anyone noticing?"

"I simply had them delivered to the back yard. I think a couple of people noticed the truck in the alley but in broad daylight nobody questioned it.

"Now, as much as I'd like to continue our little conversation, I have some work to do; ransom notes, kidnapping kinds of things. I'll return late tomorrow. You won't know exactly when so plan your escape activities accordingly. I'll leave one refill of water. I'm afraid you're going to have to make it last quite a while. Good luck."

He started to turn to leave but seemed to change his mind.

"I almost forgot something."

Closing the distance between them in a blur, he slapped her hard across the face before she could react, hurling her toward the mattress. They glared at each other for a moment in silence. Her face stung but Tanya managed to mask the pain.

"Now you know I'm still agile. I've killed so many young women like you I've literally lost count. I keep a gun and a knife on my person at all times. If you make the slightest move at me, I'll kill you without hesitation. Are we clear?"

Tanya refused to speak but he seemed satisfied he'd made his point.

Chapter 37

Sleep proved impossible, especially when attempted by force. Pills might have helped but if the ransom call came during the night he might be unable to react effectively. As the second day dawned McAllister staggered out of bed with eyes feeling like sand paper. A hot shower helped a little. Two officers fiddled with the coffee maker in the kitchen when he came downstairs; the police having been given free reign of the house. An ice cold Diet Dr. Pepper, first of the day, offered a pop as the detective wondered if the promised ransom instructions would come early or if he'd have to wait through an entire day of anguish. Would it be a phone call or a text? His worst fear was no demand would arrive at all. What if the kidnapper never made contact?

McAllister realized he didn't even know what time the mail was delivered because Tanya always took care of it. A few days of mail might already be piled up. A trip to the main gate, and the mailbox, seemed a good way to burn five minutes. A button on the wall in the kitchen beside a speaker box opened the gate. After a minute walk down the main drive something caught his eye just before he reached into the mailbox. On top of the latest deliveries of junk mail and bills a plain manila envelope perched with just 'Michael' printed in ink neatly across the front. Without touching it he ran back to the house so he could inform the police officers.

"I think I found a ransom note in the mailbox. Call the chief."

The officer was dialing the phone before he finished his sentence. Michael listened while he barked information into the phone receiver.

"The chief's talking with the FBI. They're at the station now with a full team. They'll be here pronto. You made the right call to leave the envelope alone."

Four black Chevy Suburban SUVs arrived in a flurry roughly seven minutes later. A medium-sized contingent emerged with a surprisingly young man seemingly in charge, walking straight toward Michael with a purposeful stride.

"McAllister? My name is Reilly. We'll retrieve the envelope from the mailbox immediately. I think we can do a preliminary examination here without contaminating any potential evidence. We can't waste time at this point."

Michael was relieved to find someone who presented himself as fully competent. Politics seemed to have been put aside by the law enforcement divisions. An agent spread a newspaper across the large granite countertop in the kitchen. McAllister briefly wondered where he found one because he and Tanya didn't subscribe. A technician wearing blue rubber gloves gingerly brought in the envelope, placing it on the center of the paper. Using a pocket knife he carefully slit the edge of the page-sized manila envelope and then changed to a pair of forceps to extract a single page letter inside. The note was neatly printed in very small lettering. McAllister forced his way into the pack for the first look at the list of demands.

"Michael: If you want to see Tanya alive do exactly as I say. Fill a black airplane carry-on sized suitcase with one million dollars in used twenties. I know it's a surprisingly inconsequential amount of money but it's all I need. You have one day. If you put a tracer or ink bomb with the money, I'll kill Tanya in a most inventive and painful way. I'll have instructions delivered to you tomorrow on how we will proceed. Don't bother trying to catch me at your mailbox. I'll use a more clever method of delivery next time."

The letter was signed with a large cursive "C."

"Do I need to raise a million dollars in case we need it?"

Reilly cut the detective short. "Not necessary. We have excellent counterfeit money available for use in this case, impossible to tell from the real stuff. We also have a new transmitter we can bury in the bills he'll never detect. This is a great break. We have a day to prepare. I'll pull in some reinforcements. Does anyone else have anything to say on this? I don't want to miss something here."

McAllister had spent two days feeling sorry for himself. He decided it was time to start contributing.

"I think there's a decent chance he'll mail the next letter because he said in his note he wouldn't. If he wants it here tomorrow he'll mail it today or maybe he's already mailed it. Since we know he was in town, I think he might use the main post office to make sure it gets delivered on time. I think you should station somebody down there. We should stop anyone who comes in with a manila envelope like this one and search to see if one is already there."

"That's good. We also need to check if there's any video of the post office." He nodded to one of the FBI men and held up two fingers. "What else?"

Palatine had something to say this time. "We've got several video cameras around town. I could use some help going through the tapes. We might get lucky since we know at least two of the vehicles he was using."

Reilly pointed two fingers at another agent.

Michael had another idea. "I'd like to have a look around the garage he was using in town. The place might be wiped clean but I could talk to the neighbors. I might be able to uncover something."

"Good idea, Michael, but I need you to stay here. We can't be sure he'll wait 'til tomorrow. If something develops we can't waste any time looking for you."

McAllister nodded, realizing Reilly was right. He didn't know how he was going to spend another day waiting. At least he had plenty of company. The FBI agents immediately began building a full command center in the kitchen. The note was scanned and sent electronically for further analysis.

The FBI team was preparing to disperse when Reilly's phone rang. A few short bursts of communication took place within earshot then he turned to McAllister. "Who lives next door?"

He was pointing to the estate just to the west.

"I only know him as Hal. He's been over a few times while Tanya was renovating the house. She said he would say hello sometimes when she was getting the mail."

He whispered something back into the phone. Five minutes later the phone rang again. Several of the agents hustled to the road.

"What's going on?"

"We found something in the mailbox next door. It looks like another ransom note. Agents are bringing it here for examination."

Chapter 38

Tanya shifted continuously in an effort to ease the pain in her back and sides as she sat on the mattress with her back to the wall. A broken right collarbone seemed a certainty. Reviewing the details of the room for the one hundredth time she tried desperately to find its weakness. Super sensitive to movement, light and sound after two days confined in her cell, she thought she noticed something flicker at the window. Holding her breath in anticipation she noticed a shadow flash by the window again. She quickly slid the table underneath the window and worked her way on top, a feat becoming more difficult each time she tried. Catching the burglar bar with her left hand on the first try she pulled herself up just in time to catch a glimpse of a small dog as it shot by.

"Here, boy! Come on, boy!"

The dog seemed to be a puppy, darting back and forth as he sniffed the strange odors of the plants and trees. Her arms burned as she tried to hold on to the bars but amazingly the puppy noticed Tanya's face at the window. He approached wagging his tail wildly.

"Yeah, boy. Here, boy. Where's your owner?"

The Plexiglas formed a perfect seal on the inside of the window and appeared very thick. She wasn't sure if the dog could hear her but he could definitely see her! When her arms screamed for mercy she dropped back down to the table. Flexing her hands to refresh her circulation she jumped up to the bars again, pulling herself up and this time resting her knees against the wall. The puppy had been joined by a small child playing nearby.

"Hey! Look here! Hey!"

The child was just a toddler, a young girl maybe two years old. When she saw Tanya she froze, not seeming to know what to do.

"Yes! Yes! You see me! Where's your mommy?"

Sliding down the wall again, she frantically rubbed her arms, shook them and prepared for another try. Hearing a dull voice outside, she immediately leaped again for the bars. As she pulled herself up she saw a woman scoop up the child and walk back to the sidewalk.

"Help! Help me! Look here!"

The woman continued to the sidewalk, helping the child into a stroller. The child was still looking at Tanya but her mother was oblivious, moving out of sight with the dog in tow.

"No. Come back. Here I am. Can't you see me?"

When Tanya's hands gave out she crashed down, hitting the table on her side again. She crawled back to the bed and lost all hope for a few minutes, crying inconsolably. If only she'd managed to catch the woman's attention she could be free in minutes. Eventually she regained her composure. She vowed to remain as quiet as possible in case other children played near the house. A lot of tourists visited the mission each day. While the sidewalk was probably too far away to catch their attention, it would only take one person to notice her face at the window.

She pushed the table back to the other side of the room, not wanting to leave any clue she was able to see outside. A quick inventory of the few items in the room didn't seem to offer any hope for escape. The solitary mattress might be useful if she had any means to set it on fire but at the same time a fire might do more harm than good because the smoke might be deadly. The blanket fell in the same category.

She turned to the table, a night stand with a single drawer. Sliding the drawer open to inspect it, she found a small four inch pencil with a sharp point, like the kind she remembered her dad used when he played golf, wedged at the back. Could it be used as a weapon? She thought she remembered a movie where someone used a pencil to stab a person in the neck. Unfortunately this poor idea was the best one so far. A closer examination of the table revealed four pieces that ran down the front and back, forming the framework and the legs. Could she break out one of the legs to use as a bat? It seemed a possibility, a good weapon but something only to be used as a last resort. Her captor claimed he had a gun. Was he lying? Did he always carry it?

Sliding the drawer completely out of the table, she examined it, turning it upside down in the process. A new idea seemed dangerous but worth the risk. Tanya began writing clues on the bottom of the drawer, carefully considering each item as space and pencil lead were limited. What facts could she list that could possibly help catch this man? A detailed description of the kidnapper, including his general appearance and especially the limp, seemed a good starting point. His foul odor, noticeable from some distance, was definitely noteworthy.

Two hours later the room had grown too dark to read what she was writing. As she carefully replaced the drawer and pencil, she wondered if it was a trick to leave the pencil. After an hour or so sitting on the mattress with her arms around her knees, she heard a distant click, a clear sign her senses were improving. Holding her breath she tracked his movement from what seemed the back of the house to the stairs. A few seconds later she smelled food. The slot in the door banged open but she was on to him now. Everything was done for maximum effect. He had bragged that his victims wallowed in fear. Tanya was determined to be strong.

"Lie down on the bed with your arms at your side. Do not move when I enter the room."

She complied, continuing to observe him carefully, trying desperately to notice more identifiable traits she could report. A blinding flash of light caught her completely off guard. A flashlight of some kind, much more powerful than normal, turned the cell to daylight. Not a speck of dust could find a decent hiding place.

"Let's see how you did today, shall we?"

As her eyes readjusted she watched the light dart around the room, seemingly inspecting each wall. The beam noticed scratch marks across the floor.

"I can tell you pulled the table over here under the window. You must have jumped up and caught the bars. I see marks on the wall. You pulled yourself up and saw something across the street. What was it?" Tanya worried he would realize she knew where she was but refused to respond to the question. "Oh, come on. You can tell me. You saw the mission across the street. The problem is which one because there are a lot of missions in California. Do you know how many?" She wasn't going to give him the satisfaction of playing any games. "I don't actually know the answer myself but it's something like twenty or thirty. Which one could this be? A pity you don't know. It could be any of them. You could be north of San Francisco or south in San Diego." He seemed to lose interest with his game. "You've got a few minutes to eat your dinner. Be sure and finish before I come back down."

Chapter 39

The team quickly rallied to the kitchen as the same agent hustled in with the second envelope, identical to the first one in size and color and with Michael's name printed in exactly the same fashion but this time with an address but no stamp.

"We found it in the mailbox next door. Our perp must have left this one at the same time as the other. He seems to know the routine around here pretty well. He must have waited until the mail had been delivered then left both notes. I'm sure the truck delivers to the house next door first, then here. I don't know how he managed to place these envelopes in broad daylight but I guess no one was watching yesterday; very risky behavior. This guy has balls. He must have figured the postman would notice the letter without a stamp, or the guy who owns the house would, and then notice it belonged next door."

He repeated the earlier process of opening the envelope. The letter was longer this time.

Dear Michael: I hope you enjoyed wasting your time yesterday. I wanted some play time with Tanya. I'm afraid the first note was a decoy. Here are your real instructions:

You have a Twin Mission, catch me and save Tanya. It will take you a few days to figure out who I am. Unfortunately for you I'll be long gone by then. Today I will give Tanya a large sandwich and a tall drink which will constitute her last meal. She could probably survive several weeks if she knew it was the only food and drink she was going to get.

Most likely she will consume everything immediately, as this is how I've trained her. I won't return after I have provided her this last meal. If you don't find her she'll starve to death. Let's see how good an investigator you really are, shall we? Good luck. You'll need it.'

Again it was signed with a cursive "C." The agent scanned the second note and sent it to join the first.

Michael was worried. "How in the hell are we going to find her? She could be anywhere."

Reilly didn't have an answer but seemed to try to remain upbeat. "At least we know where we stand. We also won a day. He wasn't expecting us to get this information until tomorrow's mail delivery. Maybe he'll check on us one more time today.

McAllister knew Reilly was doing the best he could but as the light faded he was losing hope. The thought of Tanya starving in a room somewhere was infuriating, especially if she was close by.

Reilly and two agents asked the detective if they could use a room for some one-on-one questioning, one last humiliation for the day. Michael knew what it was going to be about and wanted to get it over with as soon as possible. Reilly did the talking.

"Michael, I don't like this but I've got to follow procedures. As a former police investigator you should understand." He nodded. "Is there a large insurance policy on Tanya's life? Think carefully about your answer because it will only make things worse if you lie about the smallest thing."

"She didn't need life insurance. Her family has more money than most banks."

"Convince me you couldn't possibly be after her money."

"I can think of two good reasons. First, we recently decided to tie the knot. That's why she was in San Francisco. She's been planning the wedding with her mother and some of her friends." He stopped a second and gave them both a cool stare. "If I was after her money, I think I would have waited until after the wedding. As it is now, I don't have any claim to this house or any of her accounts. I also signed an agreement to that effect before we moved in together, at my insistence I might add. Her mother can verify that, too."

"What's the second good reason?"

"When my dad died he left me three million dollars. I haven't done anything with that money. I've got an old car, four pairs of cowboy boots and a couple of guitars. I'm not into collecting stuff. I piddle around writing little stories about cars for just about nothing. Tanya's shoes are worth more than everything I own."

"Go get your laptop." Michael wasn't sure where Reilly was going but he wanted to end the session as soon as possible. When he returned Reilly continued. "Pull up your investment account."

The screen showed almost three and a half million dollars in McAllister's account. His financial advisor had been doing better than expected.

"How much do you have in your checking account right now?"

"I think about twenty thousand dollars."

"Show me."

He dialed up his bank account which showed an account balance of ten million thirty-four thousand dollars and change. A few minutes were needed to explain how he'd forgotten about the ten million dollars from Peter. Reilly finally seemed to accept his explanation, possibly because it was too stupid a thing to lie about.

"I'm sorry about this, Michael. At least now when somebody upstairs says you've got to be involved, I can shut them down quickly. Do you have any idea who might've done this?"

"At first I was sure this was something to do with the De Costa case but now I don't think so. Whoever's behind this has been setting it up for a long time, well before I even met De Costa. I think it's either someone after Tanya because she's from such a wealthy family, or it's one of my old cases. I was sure it was Tanya's money, especially when we got the million dollar demand, but now it seems to me to be more about one of my old cases. The statement about seeing how good a detective I am makes me think so. What has me puzzled is all the bad guys from my old cases are dead."

"Try to get some sleep tonight. Tomorrow's going to be a big day."

Reilly left for the night but Palatine seemed to want to talk more. McAllister wanted a few minutes alone to think about the facts in the case.

"I'm going to take a little walk before I hit the sack."

Of the four agents spending the night, one looked up and quickly invited himself along when the detective headed for the door. Apparently, Michael wasn't completely off the suspect list. Retrieving a flashlight from the pantry he stepped into the cool late afternoon air with his new best friend, not certain what he was looking for. Halfway down to the creek it hit him, causing him to reverse course back to the house for the keys to the racing garage. A few minutes later he crept carefully up the stairs with the agent behind, gun drawn.

The criminal must have been observing them for some time if he knew their patterns this well. Could he possibly have been using the garage as a base, adding more insult to his crime? Fiddling with the keys, he finally opened the door and switched on the light in the front room. At first nothing seemed out of place because the bed was made and everything was just as it was the last time he saw it, but McAllister was a keen observer. Tanya kept a running joke about his awful dishes, used here in the racing garage as a leftover from his place in Tulsa. The dishes were not matched but he always left his favorite on top, even though it had a small chip in the side. Tanya had done the cooking during the months they lived there. Everyone knew he was hopeless in the kitchen. His one task was washing the dishes after each meal and he always left his favorite plate on top. It was clearly second from the top of the stack when he investigated. A small thing, yes, but something. The salt and pepper shakers were not quite in the right place, either. The room smelled a bit rank, too. He wrote that off to being closed up for so long. Deciding to keep the information about the dishes to himself for now, Michael began to realize he was up against a brazen criminal, an expert at breaking and entering and possibly with the courage to use their own garage as a vantage point. This new evidence bolstered his idea the crime had been planned for some time, but for what reason? The Tulsa killer was dead. The Slasher was dead. How could this be related to the De Costa case? Still, it was the only case left with a possible fifth man surviving. The facts didn't mesh.

On the way back to the house, the detective turned on the back patio lighting and took a slow one hundred and eighty degree look at the property. The grass near the house was kept mowed to about thirty yards. He walked to the drive then slowly scanned the edge of the lawn where it edged into the trees.

The agent asked. "What are you looking for?"

"Nothing in particular, just checking."

Michael continued to scan the woods with the flashlight in the dimming light until he reached a point near the drive that led down to the racing garage. The tall weeds were matted down, much like a spot where a deer might sleep. It looked to McAllister like the kidnapper had been lying here observing them. Had he been here the night Monroe tried to kill them? Had he watched the whole thing? Again, McAllister kept the information to himself.

Chapter 40

"Lie on your back with your arms at your side. Do this immediately. If you try anything I'll shoot you without hesitation."

The flashlight temporarily blinded her again when he entered the basement, this time searching the room in greater detail. Tanya worried he might find the writing on the bottom of the drawer. She tried desperately to control her breathing but she was losing the battle when he decided to inspect the table.

"You found the pencil. I left it in the other corner of the drawer. On second thought, maybe it just rolled over there when you were scooting the table around. I don't see anything else. How did you spend your day?"

"Why did you hit me?"

"My dear, you really must understand something. The sooner you do, the easier this will be on you. I'm not like other people you've met. The little gene that tells people right from wrong, the one that makes people feel guilty? I didn't get one. It makes no difference to me whether I kill you or not. I won't know until the last instant what I'll do. I've lost track of how many women I've raped and killed. I've killed men and children, too. It makes no difference to me."

"What's the point of kidnapping me?"

"You have a need to understand, eh? The simple truth is Michael pissed me off."

"How could Michael have possibly done anything to you?"

"I'll tell you a little story. Try to remember every detail because it will help you try to catch me if you manage to get out of this room alive. Like I said earlier, I've been a criminal for over forty years. I guess I've gotten pretty good at committing crimes. Come to think of it, I might be the best criminal who ever lived. I started sneaking into homes when I was barely a teenager. I especially enjoyed entering a house late at night when the owners were home. I used to spend hours watching them sleep. Later when I appreciated the need for money, I started robbing the houses. I wanted nice things like the other kids had. I figured out pretty quickly my parents weren't going to be providing for me very well. Of course the thrill of robbing people wasn't enough in the long run so I started raping the women. Finally, I just killed them when I was done."

His matter-of-fact manner scared Tanya. Murder seemed to him like going to get groceries.

"But what could Michael have done to you? We've never even met you before."

"I raped and killed so many women over the years in California I decided it would be best to leave for a while. The police departments started cooperating with each other, making life complicated. I tried Arizona but eventually moved across the border into Mexico. Boy, did I have some fun down there. I could move effortlessly from town to town with no chance of being caught. The cops were so incompetent it was laughable. I perfected my Spanish, too.

"A few years ago I got a little homesick so I came back to California. I'd been injured by that time so I couldn't rape women anymore. I could've murdered easily enough but I decided I didn't want the attention. I amused myself with an occasional break-in and robbery. When the Slasher started his pathetic little career I found his work interesting. He was just an amateur, of course, but I enjoyed the panic he inflicted on the state. Michael spoiled my fun. The newspapers made him out to be some kind of master detective. I decided I could give him a little more of a challenge. I want to see how good he is. I guess I'm teaching him a lesson."

Furiously making mental notes of the new information, Tanya wanted to keep him talking as long as possible.

"How did you hurt your leg?"

"I got shot if you can believe it, although I guess it was inevitable. As many homes as I've broken in to, eventually someone was bound to have a loaded gun and enough courage to use it. It happened in Mexico City. I had a heck of a time getting the bullet out. My femur was cracked but not broken. A terrible infection set in and the wound took months to heal. The bullet damaged my groin. I haven't been able to get an erection since; a lucky break for you."

"So Michael killed the Slasher and ruined your fun."

"Exactly. If he hadn't gotten involved I'd have never known you existed. I've spent the better part of the last year planning this."

"You've spent a year planning my abduction?"

"Planning is what keeps me from getting caught. I've done a lot of research. I've been inside your place in Los Gatos many times. Monroe almost screwed up my plans at the last minute."

"You were in our house in Los Gatos?"

"I've watched you and Michael sleep. I considered killing you but it would've been far too easy. You might be interested to know I've been in your mother's townhouse, too. I thought about cutting her throat and leaving you a note." Tanya had been holding herself together fairly well until his last comment. The thought of this man hovering over her sleeping mother was too much. "I decided the only way I could really hurt Michael was through you."

"Are you going to kill me?"

"Not directly, at least as long as you behave. I've given Michael some clues and of course by now he'll have the FBI helping him. If they're really good they might be able to rescue you. I doubt it but one never knows. I'm going upstairs but I'll be back down in a few minutes. We have one last little piece of business to take care of."

Tanya finally put the pieces together.

"You're the Cobra."

"Very good. Yes, I'm the Cobra. Now you know who you're dealing with. I'm the greatest master criminal this state, or the nation for that matter, has ever known."

Chapter 41

The chief stayed with McAllister well into the evening. The FBI ordered out for Chinese. McAllister certainly wasn't capable of feeding anyone. Palatine urged him to eat when the food arrived.

"You've got to keep your energy level up. I know it's a long shot but we've got to be ready if we catch a break."

Michael let his comment go but filled a plate. He hadn't eaten much during the last two days. The smell of the food caused his stomach to growl audibly.

"I've been digging on the De Costa case since you moved to San Francisco. I have an idea who's behind it. I looked into Wilson's background a little more closely and found a couple of clues. I don't want to say anything yet but it's starting to come together."

"I'm sure Tanya's abduction has something to do with one of my old cases but I can't make any connection so far. After Monroe's little escapade we tried to set up a good security system here. We knew we had to protect ourselves against criminals, even if it was just while we visited."

"That's probably why he grabbed her outside. The improvements you made to the security system made it too difficult. Somebody's been watching you all right."

Reilly entered.

"Chief, you better come with me."

"What's up?"

"It looks like the house next door was being used to keep surveillance on this house."

"I'd like to tag along if you don't mind."

Reilly was already heading out the door so McAllister decided his answer was yes. The walk to the house next door took a few minutes but it was too much trouble loading up in a bunch of trucks just to drive a hundred yards. Michael had never been inside the residence; a smaller two story. The grounds were not as expansive as the old Waldorf place, either. Agents busily combed the house and yard for evidence. McAllister and Palatine followed Reilly upstairs. The owner, Hal, an older man pushing ninety, was in a small library; possibly his study. McAllister had nodded to him a couple of times but had never engaged in a conversation. He had attended the party Tanya threw when the renovation of the house was complete. An agent seemed to have been waiting for Reilly to arrive before he started questioning him.

"Do you use this room very much?"

"Not much during the past few years. When I was working, it was my office."

"Can you remember the last time you came in the room?"

He took a minute to consider the request.

"A month or so."

Reilly gave the agent a signal.

"Okay, Hal. Thank you very much for all your cooperation. We'll be out of here in a few minutes so you can get back to your reading. We're very sorry to have disturbed you."

Michael heard Hal slowly descend the stairs. Obviously the old man didn't get around very well. When he was gone the agent turned to Reilly.

"Look over here by the window. We think someone has been using this spot for surveillance. It offers a pretty clear view of the back side of the house, the windows of the bedrooms upstairs and the drive. It would be a great place to keep tabs, especially if you wanted to know when anyone was coming or going. The furniture looks to me like it's been moved around so he could crouch near the window. I'm sure the old man wouldn't have noticed."

McAllister moved over to the window, confirming everything the agent had said with just a glance. The view looked directly at the back of the Waldorf mansion, but also showing part of the driveway. Their bedroom window was in plain view.

"You think the kidnapper had been using this house as a surveillance position without the owner knowing?"

"The old guy can hardly hear a thing and his vision is even worse. He uses about three rooms in the house. You can literally follow the trail of food crumbs to see where he goes. The kidnapper probably broke in one time to check it out then decided to make a game out of it. This guy scares me. He's not like anyone I've run into before."

His words stung McAllister's ears as he walked back to his home, confirming his earlier feeling the racing garage had also been used. He didn't like the thought of dealing with some kind of master criminal. Suddenly he felt very tired. Sleep seemed possible for the first time in two nights. His adrenaline must have hit bottom. Somehow he had to find Tanya and yet no way seemed possible. The last task on his to-do list before his head hit the pillow was a very painful call to Tanya's mom, providing a much sanitized version of what had transpired since his last call.

Chapter 42

The Cobra returned in a few minutes as he had promised, but this time he changed his routine drastically.

"I want to show you something. I must say I'm a bit proud of myself." He withdrew a smart phone from his jacket pocket. Tanya noticed it was a similar model to her own, sending her mind racing. "I shot this little video yesterday. What do you think?"

Tapping the face a few times in preparation, he handed her the phone. A video showed Michael sitting in a breakfast café in Los Gatos she knew, chatting with Palatine. Her captor had been sitting right across from Michael! She allowed the video to run its course but her mind was already working on a plan. A phone was in her hands. All she needed was a matter of seconds to send a text but even if she managed to get it off, she didn't think she would survive. How could she distract him long enough to use the phone for ten seconds?

"Pretty impressive, don't you think? I was sitting right beside your boyfriend and the police chief and they didn't have a clue. I don't think it bodes well for your chances, dear. I'm rather proud of my ability to learn how to use these new phones."

"Very impressive. Listen, I've really got to use the bathroom urgently. Can we make the same deal as yesterday?"

"Sure. Hand me the phone while I watch you strip."

Undressing slowly while keeping her back turned, she gave him plenty of time to daydream. As she walked down the hall she continued planning. Alone in a dark and filthy room she made a fateful decision. Authorities would never find her without help. If her plan failed she would probably just speed up what was going to happen anyway. After a final rehearsal in her mind, she walked back to her prison and took a deep breath.

"May I see the video of Michael one more time? It might be the last time I ever get to see him."

"Certainly. I think you might be right."

Making the request while she was still undressed, she turned her back so he could have a good view of her ass. Shaking gently as if she were crying her thumbs blazed across the tiny keyboard. Phone number. Message. Send text. Return to the video. Tossing him the phone as she scooped up her clothes, she took her time getting dressed to keep him distracted.

"Have you delivered your demands to Michael?"

"The first set. He'll get a second set tomorrow."

"Will they be something he can manage?"

"I've given him a slim chance. I can't speculate how he will do. My experience with the police does not make me optimistic."

"Michael might surprise you."

"As much as I would enjoy a challenge, I wouldn't get my hopes up if I were you."

"What are your demands for my release? You said it wasn't money."

"I can't think of a way to tell you without spoiling the fun. I'd like to, I really would, but it would ruin everything. Let's just say I've given Michael his greatest challenge as a detective.

"I have some errands to finish upstairs. I'll be back in the morning with your breakfast. I'll be gone all day tomorrow so you'll have plenty of time to consider your fate. Lie back down on the bed. You can move around when I bolt the door."

Chapter 43

Complete exhaustion flooded through McAllister's body as his head touched the pillow. Tingling as he relaxed and closed his eyes, he would have been sound asleep in less than a minute but suddenly his cell phone vibrated on the table next to the bed. Having just switched off the light he fumbled for a minute to find the switch. When he picked up the phone he couldn't believe his eyes. Screaming to the cops on the floor below, he fumbled with his jeans.

"I just got a text from Tanya. Get everybody over here."

The news spread quickly throughout the team. One of the agents had already downloaded the text to his computer before Michael even descended the stairs. In a matter of minutes several agents had gathered in the kitchen. The text was projected on a large computer screen by the time Reilly entered the room.

Sant Barbara rubio street hld in bsmnt can see twin mission towrs from window with bars

Reilly took charge.

"Get me two birds, pronto. Land them here on the lawn. I want them ready to go in fifteen minutes. Get the sheriff in Santa Barbara on the phone. Everybody get ready to move. We're out of here one minute after the choppers arrive. Pull up the area on the screen so we can have a look at Rubio Street."

McAllister grabbed Reilly's arm.

"You've got to let me go with you."

Palatine added, "Ditto for me."

"I think I can find two extra seats.

McAllister didn't realize the FBI had helicopters at the ready. When they landed he thought they were the most beautiful grey monsters he'd ever seen. He managed a short call to mom before the team lifted for the journey south.

"Tanya sent me a text."

"She escaped?"

"No, but she managed to give us her location. She's being held in Santa Barbara. We're getting ready to fly south now. I'll call you as soon as we find her."

He hung up before she could ask any more questions.

Chapter 44

Alone again in her cell, Tanya shivered nervously, not from the cold but from blind fear. If she concentrated, she could just hear the Cobra moving around the house. Turning her attention to the table she removed the drawer, furiously writing a few final notes on the bottom using a slender beam of moonlight as a guide. Calculating the Santa Barbara police would arrive in an hour, two at the most, she hoped the notes would be unnecessary but she knew things might not go as planned. A worst case scenario seemed prudent.

As she finished and replaced the drawer in the table she was sure she heard the Cobra leave through a back door. Would he would be gone until morning or return in a few minutes? The police should arrive soon. Deciding it was time to take action; she lifted the table clumsily and slammed it on the floor as hard as she could but her effort only produced a small crack along the side. Second and third tries were more successful. When she finally broke the table into pieces, she selected one of the legs and took a few practice swings as if it were a baseball bat. Next, she carefully spread the remaining pieces of the table in front of the door with the bottom of the drawer down in the hopes the Cobra wouldn't find her notes. She figured one of two things would happen: The Cobra would either make a run for it when the police showed up or he'd come back to kill her. If it was to be the latter, she was going to put up a fight. If she could catch him off balance one good swing could make all the difference.

Leaning against the wall next to the door in case he might simply try to shoot her through the slot, she tried to control her breathing. In the dead silence with minutes passing like hours, she held the leg with both hands like she was waiting on deck for the Yankees, rehearsing her moves mentally. If he was facing her, she would aim for the nose or throat. Michael mentioned once to go for the nose because it bled a lot and disoriented the attacker. If he was facing away, she'd go for the back of the head. Michael had emblazoned the most important thing about fighting to her many times; get in the first blow.

Chapter 45

Reilly was constantly sending and receiving messages through a set of headphones as they flew. McAllister tried to pick up the conversation but it was impossible with his mouth covered and the racket from the huge chopper. Reilly finally offered an update on the situation.

"We'll be in Santa Barbara in fifty minutes. The locals are cooperating fully. They're sealing off the area as I speak. We already have a sniper in one of the towers of the mission with an infrared scope. We think we can figure out the correct house in advance." He resumed his conversations for a few minutes then spoke to them again. "The note was a code. We thought there was something about the caps on Twin Mission. The mission in Santa Barbara is the only one in California with two towers. All the others have only one. I don't know how Tanya figured that out."

Michael filled him in. "She studied design at UC Santa Barbara. She probably did a project on the mission while she was in college. She would have recognized the twin towers."

Reilly nodded. "It's a huge break. We might have figured out the clues without the texting but it would certainly have taken a lot of time. We got a break on the location, too. She even got the street name right, Plaza Rubio." Showing them a device that looked like a government issued computer tablet he pulled up a map of the area around the mission then held the screen to the side so they could see it clearly. "Two sides of the mission are heavily wooded. The sniper can't see the houses where the road bends around to the south here, either. If he can't see the houses then Tanya wouldn't be able to see both towers of the mission. That leaves only this short block of eight houses across the street to the west. Four of the houses have hedges and two have walls in the front, again blocking the view of the mission from ground level. Of the remaining two houses, one is blocked by a tree. Our guy in the tower can only see a basement window on one house and it has bars on the window. We're sure it's our target."

Palatine had a good question. "What's going to happen when we get there?"

Reilly continued using the tablet, moving the map to the south with a swipe of his finger. "We're going to put down here in this school parking lot, about six blocks west. The mission is here. We'll hit the house in less than two minutes after landing. The Santa Barbara authorities have the area sealed up tight. Anyone who moves within a mile of the place will be detained and identified. In a way it's another break for us that she's locked in the basement. He's most likely not in the room with her. We'll only need five or ten seconds to get to her. We'll hit the house hard and fast so he won't have a chance to get to Tanya." He seemed to be able to tell how worried McAllister was about his girl. Reilly gripped his arm like a super hero. "We're gonna get her back. I promise you."

Michael made a valiant attempt to be convinced.

Chapter 46

Tonight was clean-up time, a process he'd repeated many times in the past. Not particularly worried about DNA or fingerprints, he simply followed a life-long procedure of removing any shred of evidence regarding his habits. Snapping on a pair of plastic gloves, he opened a large plastic trash bag and methodically collected any materials that could trace him to the house. Since he'd been using it for a little more than two years, he had more to dispose of than normal. He'd already broken his rules by using one location so long but he didn't think it would matter.

A final look through the first floor confirmed he hadn't missed anything. In the morning he'd buy Tanya her last meal, then leave for good. It was a pity he couldn't watch her die. Maybe he'd come back in a few months if they didn't find her. He doubted they would. Hoisting the plastic bag over his shoulder, he carefully opened and closed the back door as he left so Tanya would not hear his movements.

The trash bag could not be discarded in the bin behind the house; obviously the first place the cops would search. Remaining in the shadows as he moved down the alley, he tried to think of an explanation in case he ran into a resident walking a dog. Possessing a thorough knowledge of the area, he planned to walk six or seven blocks before he'd dump the bag into a trash container, maybe even a little farther this last time. Moving north across a large parking area used as over-flow by visitors to the mission, he entered a small wooded area before reentering another group of houses to the west.

When he was almost a mile from the house a police cruiser shot down the street silently, setting off alarm bells in the criminal's mind. A car traveling at high speed with no lights or siren seemed odd. Luckily he was still in the shadows when it passed. He waited a moment to make sure the coast was clear then crossed to the next alley. Halfway up the block he heard and then caught a glance between the houses of two more police cars repeating the performance of the first. One car could have been a chance occurrence but three cars couldn't be a coincidence. How had they figured out his location?

Standing in the moonlight he retraced the last day in his mind. The cell phone! He'd put the damn thing in her hands himself! How in the hell did she know where she was? The mission? Yes, she could see it from the window but how would she know she was in Santa Barbara? Maybe it was the cell phone signal itself; somehow giving away his location. He'd have to figure it out later.

Years of experience served him well. A getaway car was parked a full two miles away from the house. Dropping the trash bag in the nearest container, he quickly disassembled the cell phone and crushed the pieces, jamming his heel hard against the components on a cement drive. He tossed the pieces into the container with the rest of the trash.

His habit of wearing a backpack containing his computer and supplies each time he left the house served him well. The smart move would be to proceed to his car for a sure escape but he couldn't let go of the fact Tanya had outsmarted him. If he tried to get back to the house avoiding the police would be difficult but not impossible. And he could teach her a lesson.

Chapter 47

Police vehicles of every description littered the parking lot of an old school building as McAllister exited the gray beast the moment it landed. An ambulance caught him by surprise, something he hadn't allowed himself to consider. Two male attendants stood at the ready, one nervously smoking a cigarette. Quickly shifting back to the positive the detective reminded himself they'd caught an unbelievable break. It seemed possible he could have Tanya back in minutes. The bark of Reilly's orders to a shadowy group of large, grim-faced men announced the wait was over.

An agent pulled McAllister to the side, pointing up the road to a building illuminated by spotlights and surrounded by a large park, the mission, but he couldn't see any towers from his vantage point a few blocks away. Reilly shouted into a mouthpiece extending from a helmet he'd donned, asking the sniper if he'd seen movement in the target house. The answer seemed negative.

A second local team was already positioned by the entrance to an alley, sealing off any possible escape. The Cobra seemed to be cornered. Reilly shouted a final command and his team sprinted down the street for the assault. From what McAllister had overheard, the mission was illuminated but the lights all pointed toward the building, leaving their target in relative darkness. A sniper in one of the towers across the street could easily cover the front of the house so the assault team planned to crash through the back door. Palatine was ordered to stay behind with McAllister. One minute seemed like an hour but finally an FBI agent in communication with the assault team pointed at McAllister and pulled an imaginary trigger just as a bang sounded in the distance. The agent reported a salvo of tear gas pellets had been fired through the window.

"They're in." A minute passed by. "Nobody on the first floor. They're going down to the basement." Another minute. "They found the cell! What?" The cruel expression he gave McAllister left no doubt something had gone wrong. "You'll have to stay here while they investigate."

Palatine made a vain attempt to grab the detective but no human was going to stop McAllister as he sprinted toward the mission. Cowboy boots didn't make the run easy but in seconds he made a hard right down the alley towards the team of agents illuminated two houses down. As he approached the house he met the first ring of police. "You can't. . ." Not even slowing he brushed past the first two officers. When he reached the back yard he encountered more FBI agents but managed to get past them because they were looking towards the house. Taking the three steps of the small back porch in a single leap, he bolted inside the house, still filled with toxic smoke. Teargas burned his eyes as he searched for the stairs to the basement, finally sliding more than running down. At the entrance to a hallway two large armored men grabbed him firmly by each arm. Reilly came out of a room with a desperate look on his face.

"I failed you, Michael. We were too late."

"What do you mean, too late?"

"She's gone."

"She's dead?"

"She's not here."

"Let me see."

Pushing his way into a room packed with agents and flashlight beams darting in all directions, he immediately noticed blood on the floor. Turning to Reilly he took command.

"Give me one of those flashlights. I did a lot of hunting with my dad when I was a kid. I'll find her."

Following a trail of blood droplets, he stopped to train the light on a large bloody knife on the third step so the agents would see it and then continued. Tracing the blood through the kitchen and out the back door was easy but he lost it momentarily in the grass of the back yard. Bolting to the alley he quickly picked up the trail again but it diverged, some to the left, more to the right. With no time to waste he spun back to Reilly.

"There's more blood heading to the right so the trail will be easier for you to follow. I'll go the other way."

Now only droplets dotted the rough pavement but he could follow the trail at a fast walk. Two houses down it disappeared so he backtracked to a house on the other side of the alley. A back gate displaying a small bloody hand print at the top told him he was on the right path. Instantly deciding to head to the drive on the right of the house he couldn't pick up the blood trail on the pavement. Reversing back around the house to the left side he found another gate with a bloody print. More grass led to the sidewalk on the next street but he couldn't find any blood. Heading back to the gate he noticed a series of bushes forming a hedge with some broken branches about half way down. Pushing through he found Tanya lying on her back. McAllister turned to an agent who had been trailing him.

"Get that ambulance down here now!"

She moaned softly as he scooped her up in his arms. "I'm so sorry. I'm so sorry."

Gently laying her on the grass by the street he unbuttoned the bloody bottom of her blouse, revealing a nasty knife wound in her lower stomach. Covering the wound with his hand, the ambulance arrived in under a minute. When he tried to enter the truck the attendant barred the door.

"We've got to work on her en route to the hospital. You'll be in the way. Meet us there."

The door slammed in his face as the ambulance spun its tires, a siren beginning its obnoxious song and illuminating the confused faces of the neighbors as they poked their heads out to see what was happening. A couple of Santa Barbara deputies materialized, one of them nodding toward McAllister.

"Come with us. We'll give you a ride to the hospital."

McAllister pointed out Palatine at the end of the block so he could join them. The deputy drove fast but not as fast as the detective wanted him to. When they arrived at the hospital the deputy seemed to know his way around, directing them through a maze of hallways to a room where a nurse was waiting.

"We took Miss Stafford straight to surgery. Undoubtedly she has internal injuries. There's no way of knowing how long she'll be in the operating room. It could be morning before we can tell you anything."

Her shoes squeaked on the floor as she turned and disappeared.

McAllister mumbled to no one in particular. "I guess I better call Tanya's mother and give her an update."

"She already knows."

"What do you mean?"

"The Santa Barbara sheriff told me he had orders to keep her posted. I guess if you're a billionaire you have some pull."

The deputy somehow disappeared, leaving Palatine and McAllister to bravely make small talk for thirty minutes. Even after a search for a bad cup of coffee it had only been an hour when they returned to the waiting room. Slumping into chairs designed for maximum torture they both managed to dose off as the adrenaline rush from the past few hours wore away. A movement in the waiting room jolted McAllister awake but he was disoriented and not sure if he'd slept ten minutes or ten hours. A clock on the wall said six. Just as he shook Palatine, three men strode into the room and expertly formed a wall of dark suits.

"Michael McAllister?" He nodded. "You've been served."

One of the men grabbed his arm and slapped a fat envelope into his hand.

"What's this?"

"A restraining order. You are not to call Mrs. Stafford or try to contact her in any way. You are not to be within five hundred feet of her at any time. You are forbidden to attend the funeral in San Francisco."

"What funeral?"

"Miss Stafford passed away on the operating table early this morning."

"Like hell she did."

"She passed away two hours ago. Her remains are already on a plane heading back to San Francisco. You've got two weeks to remove yourself and your belongings from the residence in Los Gatos. Anything you own in San Francisco will be delivered to Los Gatos tomorrow. You are not to take any property belonging to the Stafford family."

McAllister decided to start the grieving process by beating the hell out of the one who was doing the talking but Palatine stepped between them.

"Okay boys, you've done your job. It's time for you to leave. If you want any trouble you'll need to go get some more guys. Three of you won't be enough."

They turned and disappeared in unison. McAllister looked at Palatine in disbelief.

"I don't believe them. I'm going to find that nurse. Why didn't she wake me up?"

McAllister made an ass of himself with the first three staffers he found with Palatine serving as a witness. When each reported the same story he finally began to think the impossible might be true. Sinking to his knees he started to cry, babbling nonsense while Palatine pretended it was meaningful. Finally he looked to Palatine from his knees.

"How can you get a restraining order in the middle of the night?"

"We need to figure out how to get back home, Michael."

The chief spoke privately to the nurse for a moment, then reached down with a giant hand, catching McAllister under the arms and pulling him to his feet. When they exited the emergency room a different police officer seemed to be waiting for them.

"May I give you a ride somewhere?"

Palatine took charge. "I guess we need to go to the airport."

"I have clearance from my chief to take you anywhere you wish. I would consider it a privilege."

"Los Gatos is a long drive."

Palatine rode up front with the Santa Barbara officer after he insisted McAllister take a couple of pills the nurse had given him. The detective didn't pass out but he bounced around on the back seat in a semi-conscious dream world. Tanya was already turning into a picture in a magazine; a girl he never really had for his own. Arriving back at the Waldorf place just as the sun cleared the mountains the next morning; they found Palatine's truck waiting patiently. The chief came inside after Michael unlocked the door.

"Do you have any sleeping pills?"

"I think there's some in the bathroom upstairs."

"Go get 'em."

When McAllister returned with the bottle he asked. "Don't you have some at home?"

"They're not for me, dumbass. Take two while I'm here with you."

McAllister did as ordered. "I'm going to find the guy who did this."

The chief nodded. "I'm going to help you, too, but right now you need to rest. Call me when you wake up. I'll try to have some information for you."

Chapter 48

When McAllister awoke he found himself disoriented by the powerful narcotics. For a few seconds everything was okay. The pillow next to his head still held Tanya's scent. Then he remembered everything. The clock on the nightstand said three. Light streaming through the window told him it was afternoon. Two powerful sleeping pills had only yielded a few hours of sleep. Lying in bed for a few minutes he tried to test theories about who could be behind the abduction and murder. When nothing made sense he gave up.

Heading downstairs to quench a sudden urgent thirst he was greeted by loud snoring coming from the living room. He found Palatine lying in a heap, his shirt tail pulled out in disarray, exposing a white freckled belly.

"Chief, wake up." Palatine gathered himself awkwardly, swinging his feet over the side of the couch so he could sit up as he rubbed his face. "Why didn't you go home?"

"I was worried about you. I didn't think you should be alone." McAllister considered the chief's comment. "I've got a good reason to stay alive for now. When I find the guy who killed Tanya, that's when you need to start worrying about me. I won't have a reason in the world to stay alive after I take care of him." McAllister gave the chief a pat on the shoulder.

"I better head home and reintroduce myself to the wife. In the next few days I'm going to need a favor from you. I think I can close the book on the De Costa case and get you going on Tanya's case, if you think you could start trusting me. By the way, have you taken me off the suspect list yet?"

McAllister ignored his question but replied. "I'll give you a day or two before I start poking my nose where you won't like it. Keep in mind I'm not a patient man."

The chief seemed to know better than to argue with McAllister. After a wave as the chief drove out the gate, Michael was alone. No, he wasn't just alone; he was the loneliest man on the planet. For a minute he allowed himself to wish he'd never come to California, that Peter Stafford had never found Lucille, that his father had never bought the Jag. Convincing himself Tanya would have died the first night he met her if he hadn't come to the party didn't help. They'd had more than a year together, less than two. His time with Tanya had saved him from his demons. His mind drifted for just a moment to the sleepless nights searching for a serial killer in Tulsa, realizing the nightmares would be returning; only this time they would be much worse.

The only cure was to get busy. His full time job would be to find out who killed Tanya, requiring every waking moment; his only purpose for living. What could he do today, this minute, to solve the case? The house next door had been used by the killer but it didn't seem to offer much because the kidnapper didn't live there. Palatine couldn't help him, yet. One thing was for sure, he wasn't going to accomplish anything sitting in the house.

Lucille started faithfully and strong. McAllister was surprised by a gang of reporters gathered outside the property. He slammed his foot down hard on the accelerator as the gate opened, spraying gravel in all directions and scattering the crowd amid curses as he flew by.

Arriving at his destination in minutes, he surprised himself at his ability to find the garage used by the kidnapper without too much trouble. As the gravel crackled under Lucille's tires in the alley he wondered what he thought he could possibly find at the abandoned garage in the way of clues. The killer had cleaned the building thoroughly making it doubtful he'd find any evidence inside. The neighbors and shops in the area seemed to be the only chance to glean any new information. The garage was the first building on the block with a series of industrial buildings extending down one side of the alley. Normal houses lined the other side of the alley. The last few days had been such a whirlwind he realized he didn't know what day it was, or for that matter if it was a weekday or weekend. Guessing a week day he turned toward the industrial buildings even though it was almost five. A voice from behind startled him.

"May I take a picture of your car?"

He spun around quickly, reaching inside his jacket for the handle of his gun. Now it was a girl's turn to be startled, about ten years of age as far as McAllister could guess. The little girl looked straight out of a cute Girl Scout cookie commercial but he had no time to waste.

"Why do you want to take a picture of my car?"

"I love cars. I take pictures of them all the time. I haven't taken pictures of a car like this, though. What is it?"

"You don't have a camera."

"I use my cell phone, silly." She pulled a slender smart phone from the front pocket of her jeans.

McAllister was about to say something very stupid to end the conversation when something dawned on him.

"May I ask your name?"

"Sherry."

"Sherry, my name is Michael. Did you ever take any pictures of the man who used this garage?"

"Of course. He owned four cars."

"Did you take pictures of all of them?"

"Yes, but he was an asshole."

McAllister was surprised by the adult nature of the young girl, but he knew he had gotten lucky. "Why do you say that?"

"One day when he came here the door was up on the garage for a few minutes, the first time I'd seen it open. I saw the four cars inside so I asked him if I could take pictures of them but he said no. He pushed me out and closed the door. I fooled him, though. I took pictures of him later through a hole in the fence over there."

"Is that your house?"

"Yes."

"We need to have a talk with your mother."

Convincing her mother he was working with the Los Gatos police proved a little difficult at first because he didn't have any identification to prove it. The little girl, although only ten, acted more like twenty. McAllister decided to be blunt. Mother and daughter sat together on the sofa while he addressed them.

"I'm a detective helping the Los Gatos police. I'm working on a big case. You should know it's a murder case." Her mother gasped when he said the word murder but the girl narrowed her eyes and concentrated. Just pronouncing the words turned him cold inside when he thought about Tanya. "We're sure the man who was using the garage out back was the murderer. The pictures Sherry took could prove to be a tremendous help to us in the investigation. I need to see the pictures of the cars. I also need to see if you have any good shots of the man."

Sherry retrieved a laptop computer from her bedroom, setting it up on a table in the kitchen. She quickly and expertly found a file containing the pictures he was after. The file of interest contained over one hundred pictures, taken over a period of several months. The quality of the photos proved difficult to assess. The cell phone didn't seem to have a very strong zoom feature.

"Would you by any chance have a memory stick? I need to copy these pictures so I can study them."

"I have a brand new one. I just bought it."

She shot back to her room and reappeared with a high quality memory stick still in the box; copying the files in a matter of minutes.

"Here's forty dollars for you to replace your memory stick, including your gas and time. Are we good?" Sherry nodded. "I'll keep in touch with you. In the meantime watch the newspapers. These pictures might make you famous."

McAllister started to race home and begin work on the pictures but paused. Looking down at the shifter he spoke to his new partner.

"So, Lucille, you've decided to help on the case. You found us a witness. Good work. I'm going to need all I can get."

Studying the pictures on his laptop at home long into the night he found multiple pictures of all four of the vehicles. The police already had plenty of information on the truck and the car he'd used when he kidnapped Tanya. The other two cars were the treasure trove. The question was whether the police could enhance the images enough to get a good license plate number or a clear shot the suspect's face.

McAllister arrived at the station at nine sharp the next morning and asked to see the chief. His admin had bad news.

"He's not going to be in today but he'll check in regularly. He said he's working on something important."

McAllister decided against leaving a message, preferring to talk to him off the record. As he prepared to leave he noticed Stacy Carson's office door beckoning. Her face lowered when he entered her domain.

"Michael, I'm so sorry about Tanya."

He plowed ahead because he had no good response for her. "I found some new information yesterday. It needs to be forwarded to the FBI as soon as possible but the chief's not around today."

"I can take care of it. What did you find?"

"You won't believe this. A young girl, who lives across the alley from the garage that was rented by the kidnapper, happens to be a photography buff who absolutely loves to take pictures of cars. She took over a hundred pictures of the garage with each of the cars and the killer. I've got them on this memory stick."

"Let me copy it. I'll process the data and forward it to the FBI. Palatine called me early this morning. He said he wouldn't be in but to call him if something came up. I'll take care of everything for you. I'll make sure these pictures get the attention they deserve."

"Thanks. Ask Palatine to call me when he gets a chance." McAllister started to leave but changed his mind. "You know I'm going after this guy. I might need some information from time to time on an unofficial basis, if you know what I mean."

"I'll get you anything you need. Call me anytime, day or night. I'll always be here for you."

McAllister considered her choice of words as he headed back to Lucille.

Chapter 49

McAllister got nothing more than promises from the chief over the next two days. He continued to grind on the pictures of the cars but wasn't making significant progress. The FBI didn't feel the need to share anything with him, either. The gloom of a thick morning fog seemed fitting on the third day. The time and place of Tanya's funeral hadn't been too difficult to find using his computer. No legal papers were going to keep him away. After shining his black boots he dressed in his best jeans and swung on a leather jacket. Just as he was preparing to leave his cell phone rang.

"Open the gate."

Michael walked out back to greet Palatine as he entered the property.

"Have you finally got something for me?"

"Tomorrow."

"You've been putting me off with that answer for days. I want to get to work finding out who did this. You've got to give me something."

"I promise you tomorrow you're going to get everything."

"What are you here for now?"

"I'm going with you to the funeral. I want to make sure you don't get yourself in trouble. I think a badge might be helpful."

In truth McAllister was relieved the chief would be with him. Palatine drove his police truck because his GPS made it easy to find the location, parking on the opposite side of a large crowd already gathered at the cemetery. They remained by the truck at a distance from the proceedings with Michael hoping Tanya's mother wouldn't even notice he'd attended. After a few minutes the three men who had served McAllister walked towards them. The same one did the talking.

"I thought I make it clear you were not to attend the funeral. I'm going to call the police and have you removed."

Palatine cut Michael off before he could blow his stack.

"We are the police. We're over five hundred feet away from Mrs. Stafford. We're not here to cause any trouble. You boys need to head back before I decide to quit playing nice."

Scowling as they left, they seemed to realize Palatine was a mountain they weren't ready to climb.

"Thanks." Somehow it still seemed possible McAllister would wake up from a dream until a white coffin came out of the back of a hearse, proving to be the ultimate reality. McAllister convulsed and threw up in the street. "Get me out of here."

Palatine nodded. Michael knew where she was now. He'd come back when he could be alone with her. Palatine surprised him on the drive back.

"I'll need that favor tomorrow. I'd rather not say right now what it's about. You'll have to trust me. It could be dangerous so I'll return your gun." He didn't bother to mention with Tanya dead there was no need for any evidence on the Monroe death.

"Wear the same jacket you've got on now so you can hide it, but don't hide it too much. There's a chance you'll have to use it."

McAllister nodded. Reasons for danger or gunplay weren't necessary anymore. Dying wasn't something he feared.

"I have to get a few things lined up. I'll call you a few minutes before I pick you up. It should be right after lunch. When we're done with my little errand I'll give you everything we have on Tanya's case. You'll have plenty to keep you busy."

Busy sounded good.

Chapter 50

The next morning the chief was good on his word for a change. As McAllister finished a piece of peanut butter toast, something he pretended was lunch, his cell phone rang.

"Come down to the station. I'll drive from here."

Grabbing an ice cold can of Diet Dr. Pepper for the road; he found the chief waiting by the truck when he arrived at the back of the station. They headed west to Santa Cruz then south along the coast. After forty minutes McAllister decided they were going to Monterey.

Palatine sat in icy silence for most of the trip. All McAllister cared about was the information he was going to get when they were done. The chief finally offered some instructions as they reached the outskirts of Monterey.

"We're heading to a residence. We'll meet with a husband and wife. Back me up no matter what happens." Palatine took his eyes off the road momentarily and gave the detective a cold stare. "Be ready to shoot to kill because this man is very good with a gun. I'm going to try to convince him he has a lot to lose by putting up a fight but he might not agree. If there's shooting, he'll go for me first. If he does, kill him. Don't try anything fancy. If he causes any kind of trouble shoot him.

"If we need a story for the police just say I needed something on the De Costa case. No matter what anyone asks you just say that, nothing more."

The instructions were clear enough. A week ago McAllister would have wondered what the man had done. Was he the fifth man? How did Palatine know for sure? Now he didn't care. If Palatine said to shoot him, he'd shoot him.

When the welcome sign for Monterey came and went, McAllister wondered if they might be heading to Pebble Beach but the chief turned at the Pacific Grove exit. He pulled the big SUV in front of a small house in a well-groomed neighborhood; one of those areas where the tiny houses built fifty years before were slowly being razed so new billionaires could build castles. The little house backed up to a golf course, not a fancy one like Pebble Beach, but more like a public course for semi-normal golfers, in case any existed in Monterey. Palatine led them to the front door. The woman who answered didn't seem very threatening.

"Sean. What a surprise. It's so good to see you. What's going on?"

"I need to see Dave. I'm afraid I need some advice."

"He's out for a drive but he should be home any second. Please come in. I'll make you a coffee while you wait."

Shown to an octagonal room with the back half made up of windows looking out to the golf course, Palatine motioned for McAllister to sit beside him so they could keep their backs to the windows and face the front door. McAllister turned sideways for a moment and noticed the ocean in full view about a mile away. A voice came from the kitchen.

"Sean, have you seen Dave's new toy?"

"No."

"He went and bought an old Corvette about six months ago, a nineteen sixty seven model. He's always wanted one but this one is really fixed up fancy."

The chief seemed like he was preparing a response when a roar came from the garage on the other side of the kitchen.

"There he is now. Why don't you come out and see it."

The woman led them through a doorway to the garage so tiny Palatine had to stoop to get through. The Corvette had been turned off when they arrived but the engine popped from the heat. A smallish, very fit man sat in the driver's seat with a broad smile on his face.

"Sean. What brings you here?"

"I need to ask you about a case that's got me puzzled. I guess I need some of your sage advice."

"I don't think I can teach you much anymore but I'll help you in any way I can."

As they maneuvered their way back inside he offered his hand to McAllister.

"I'm Dave Speer, police chief in Monterey. Sean used to work for me."

"My name's McAllister."

His face showed he recognized the name. He didn't seem too pleased to make the detective's acquaintance. All four of them sat at the table while the two police chiefs made small talk. Speer seemed to know something was up, eyeing McAllister nervously a couple of times. Michael made sure his jacket was open so Speer could see his gun. Surely Speer wouldn't try anything with his wife in the room. Finally Palatine got down to business.

"Dave, this is police business."

Speer seemed to get the message.

"Mary, would you please take these dishes into the kitchen so we can talk privately?"

She acted like it wasn't the first time something like that had happened and quietly disappeared. The three men stared at each other for almost a minute before Palatine broke the silence.

"Just tell me why, Dave?"

Speer could only manage a worried laugh.

"Why what?"

"Why you got yourself mixed up with Monroe and this De Costa case. How could you be so stupid?"

Speer's eyes blazed when he spoke in a low determined tone, like a wolf backed into a corner.

"How dare you come into my house and accuse me of being a criminal. Mary and I have been like parents to you. I want you out of here now. I'll never forgive you for this."

"The only place I'll go from here is downtown to file charges against you and I've got plenty of evidence to back me up. I wouldn't have come here if I didn't. There's a copy of everything sitting on my desk, too, in case you feel like trying something. That's why I brought McAllister with me. We're not fooling around."

"Evidence of what? You've got nothing."

Palatine gave him a cold stare and continued. "Think about what a trial in this town would do to your reputation. Maybe there's one chance in ten you might beat the rap but I wouldn't count on it. Most importantly, a trial would kill Mary. She'd find out everything and lose all respect for you. Even if you won, she'd know."

McAllister watched a man accept defeat in a matter of a few seconds. Fear showed in his eyes as the blood drained from his face. Experience reminded the detective when a dangerous man got scared, somebody usually got hurt. He slowly moved his hand to the butt of his gun while Palatine continued.

"Again, Dave, my question is why? You've got a good life here. You've got this fantastic house with a million dollar view. You're just about ready for a fat pension. Why would you risk all of this? I don't get it?"

A resigned man spat out the words. "Did you see the house across the street when you pulled up?"

"You mean that monster they just framed?"

"Yeah, that one. They spent a million on the old house then tore it down and spent another million on the new one."

"You've got a nice place here."

"It's a damn cracker box compared to what these rich guys build. I'm tired of them laughing behind my back. I wanted to live the good life like them so I started making some money on the side. Monroe heard about a card game in Monterey almost a year ago. De Costa supposedly took a guy for fifty grand so we did some investigating. We thought he might have a lot of money in the safe at his house; maybe a million dollars. With that kind of money I could build a nice house here like the one across the street."

He buried his face in his hands and without looking up he asked Palatine a question, the same one McAllister had in mind.

"How'd you figure it out?"

"The first time I knew for sure was when you bought the Corvette."

"The Corvette?"

"Wilson bought one, too. Not as nice as yours but the same model, just the kind of thing somebody does when he wants to emulate his boss. That's when I knew for sure. I also ran a little trace on your cell phone the night Reed hung himself. You got a call when he was brought in. You were smart enough not to take your cell phone with you when you went to the jail but the call was still there. You knew Reed was in your jail. The next thing anybody knew, Reed was dead."

"How in the hell did you get a warrant for my phone records without me knowing about it?"

"I worked in this town a long time before I moved to Los Gatos. I've got some connections here, too."

Another uncomfortable pause lasted almost a minute.

"Is there anything I can do to fix this?" Speer looked nervously at McAllister then back at Palatine.

"There's only one way you can come out of this without losing your reputation, your pension and Mary's respect."

"Tell me. I'll do anything."

"There's only one way, Dave. There's only one way for me to have justice and to cover this up. Think about it."

Shaking his head from side to side slowly his demeanor suddenly calmed. "You'll make sure Mary is taken care of?"

"If you do what needs to be done, I'll cover up everything so she can get your pension. It's the only way you can go out on top."

After a few seconds he solemnly nodded his head. Palatine grabbed Speer's arm as he got up from the table.

"Don't try anything. We'll do what we have to do. Call Mary back in here to sit with us."

McAllister interrupted. "What about Tanya? Did you have anything to do with her?"

Speer spat out his reply. "Waters was dead. Monroe got rid of Wilson. We had a patsy with Reed. Monroe was the only one who worried me because he wasn't above blackmail. Tanya took care of the main problem I had left. When Reed presented himself I was home free. I didn't have to split the money and nobody was left to talk. I had no reason to go after Tanya. All I wanted was for everybody to forget about the case."

Palatine thought of something else. "Where's the money you stole from De Costa?"

"You're not getting it. That's part of the deal."

Palatine hesitated then nodded. McAllister guessed the chief figured the money wasn't worth pursuing.

Speer called to his wife. "Mary?" Her head appeared around the corner. "Come back and sit with these gentlemen while I put on my uniform. I'm afraid I've got to go downtown. Sean needs to look at some evidence down at the station. It looks like some more things have turned up on Monroe. I'll try to take care of it as fast as I can. I swear I don't know how much more of this I can take. He's been a huge embarrassment to the department."

While Palatine made small talk with Mary, McAllister removed his gun, holding it underneath the table, halfway expecting Speer to fly around the corner at any moment with his gun blazing. What seemed like an eternity probably lasted five minutes. Finally a huge explosion rocked the house. Mary screamed. Palatine instinctively drew his gun and started giving orders.

"Michael, go check the back of the house. I'll stay here with Mary. Be careful."

Crossing a living room dressed in a big screen television and a sagging leather sofa, McAllister noticed a hallway beckoning on the other side. The first room on the left was a small bedroom but it was empty. Inching his way down the hall, another bedroom appeared at the end. Finger on the trigger of his pistol and ready for anything, the detective took a quick peek into the room. Still no sign of Speer. Another door to the left opened to a bathroom. After a quick glance inside, McAllister holstered his gun. Speer was lying on his back in the tub in full dress uniform. Blood spatter covered the tiles above and was just starting to run down the drain.

The first Monterey Police unit arrived in less than ten minutes. The authorities gave up questioning McAllister after an hour. When he walked out the front door for some fresh air, the sun was low on the horizon. Noticing the framed house that had caused all the trouble across the street, he walked over for a closer look, wandering aimlessly through the naked structure as he tried to figure out the purpose of each room. Eventually he made his way up the stairs and found a seat between two studs on the edge of the second floor with his legs dangling over the side. The sun was setting brilliantly over a dark bank of clouds near the horizon. The expensive view was the same as the small house across the street. Speer had lost everything because he felt he wasn't rich enough. McAllister had worked as a special investigator for the Tulsa police for twenty years. His salary the last year was ninety five thousand dollars and he felt truly wealthy. With no debt, he wouldn't have had to work anymore even without the inheritance from his dad or the money from Peter Stafford. He could have afforded to buy his friends a beer or lunch whenever he felt like it. What more did a man need?

When he met the Staffords, he found out a little about how billionaires lived. Yes, they had better clothes and toys but their lives were no better than his. The endless pursuit of money seemed insane.

After another hour Palatine escaped. Surveying the street for a minute he noticed Michael, waving at him to come down. The two lawmen rode in silence for a full fifteen minutes before the chief finally spoke.

"Do you think I was wrong to do what I did?" McAllister continued to stare ahead at the grey ribbon of road. "It was the only way I could keep Speer's pension for Mary. They'll make him a hero in Monterey. I told the investigators he felt Monroe had embarrassed the department. I tried to sell them on the idea Speer cracked up because one of his own men was involved in the De Costa murders." The chief seemed to be trying to justify the whole thing. When he looked at McAllister for approval the detective refused to bite.

McAllister's take was pretty simple. "Reed tried to use Monroe to get an angle on old man De Costa. Monroe probably decided early on he was going to kill Reed. It was just a matter of finding the right time and place. Ditto for Wilson and Waters. The funny thing is Monroe was always going to get it too, from Speer. If Monroe had just gone after Reed instead of me and Tanya, Speer might have pulled this whole thing off. In the end, every one of them turned out to be morons."

"Look, I'm sorry I used you back there."

"I don't care about the De Costa case anymore. I don't care if Speer was the mastermind. I don't care about any of it."

"I needed someone outside the department who could keep his mouth shut."

"All I want is the information you have on Tanya's killer. I'm going to use it to find him. It'll be the only thing on my mind tonight, tomorrow and every day after."

"Good. It played out the way I hoped. Let's go to the station. I've got a lot to show you."

Chapter 51

A glance at his watch told McAllister it was after eight when they pulled up behind the station in Los Gatos.

"Wait here. I'll just be a minute." The chief returned with a manila envelope. "Let's go get something to eat. I'll explain what's here over dinner."

"One small envelope doesn't seem like much information to me. You said you had a lot to keep me busy."

"Several discs inside this envelope are packed with data. Believe me; you'll have plenty to go through."

McAllister regretted the choice of the Los Gatos Bar and Grill when they pulled up, instantly remembering the last time he visited with Tanya, but he was too tired to argue. Finding a quiet table in the corner, the chief wouldn't start until they ordered.

"First of all, the identity of Tanya's killer is known."

"Let's go get him."

"I'm afraid it won't be quite that easy. The man who killed Tanya was the Cobra."

The news was so stunning McAllister couldn't comment for almost a minute.

"That doesn't seem possible. I thought he was dead."

"We did too but he left his DNA on the envelope, remember? The DNA was a perfect match for the Cobra."

"I studied some of his files when we were trying to build a profile of the killer in Tulsa. The Cobra case was the prototype for

DNA databases in the nineties. Didn't he get started in the seventies?"

"Yes, then in the early nineties he disappeared. The authorities thought he died, maybe got himself killed in a car wreck or something stupid like that. The FBI lab found plenty of DNA in his case files. There's absolutely no doubt it's a match to several pieces of evidence in Tanya's case." Palatine paused a minute before he continued. "Some of this is pretty rough. I hope you can handle it. I say let's get through it right now so you can get on with your investigation."

"Nothing could be worse than the situation I'm in now."

"Don't be so sure about that. The room where Tanya was held was practically bare, containing only a mattress and a small table."

"Had she been . . . ?"

"Without an autopsy we'll never know. Evidence in the basement led us to believe Tanya put up a pretty good fight. Authorities found a lot of blood on one of the legs of the table as well as some small hair fibers. The thinking was Tanya slammed the Cobra in the face when he entered the basement, catching him either across the nose or in the eyes. He left a considerable amount of his blood in the basement, up the stairs, outside on the porch and in the alley. I think she hurt him pretty badly. Blood and hair samples stuck to one of the legs of the table were a definite match to the Cobra. Detectives also found detailed information Tanya had apparently written on the bottom of the drawer to the table. She observed the killer carefully then wrote notes to help us, even identifying him as the Cobra. I'm not sure if she figured it out or if he told her. She described his appearance in great detail. She said he'd been in Mexico since he disappeared from California. Apparently he came back for a visit while the Slasher thing was going on. When you tracked down the Slasher and killed him, the Cobra decided to teach you a lesson. You'll find a ton of pictures of the crime scene. The notes on the bottom of the drawer make me think she knew her chances of getting out weren't good."

"So Tanya's mother was right about me getting her killed. It was just the Slasher case instead of De Costa."

"The Cobra was a deranged serial killer. Nothing he's done makes sense to normal people. It wasn't your fault."

Palatine tried valiantly but they both knew Michael would be carrying the guilt of her death for the rest of his life.

"Tanya really impressed the police officers and the FBI, pulling herself up so she could see out the window and figuring out where she was. She managed to get his cell phone long enough to send a message but that must have been a pretty good trick, too. She almost pulled off an impossible escape. I don't think we'd have ever found her if she hadn't helped us; quite a girl.

"There's one more thing she wrote on the bottom of that drawer that we have to talk about. I'm going to give it to you straight so take a deep breath. She was pregnant."

The room flashed white. The information hit the detective in the gut like a kick from a mule. For the first time it made sense why Tanya and her mother were so happy the last day in San Francisco. The safety of their unborn child was the reason for the desperate need to move back to San Francisco. Michael glowed with pride when he thought how valiantly she'd fought to save herself and their child.

"Her mom didn't allow an autopsy but we know because she visited a doctor in town the day you drove to Los Angeles. The doctor's visit must have been the first time she was sure. The doctor's report estimated she was about three months pregnant. Now we know why her mother wouldn't allow an autopsy. Funny, a billion dollars really streamlined police procedure. I assumed you didn't know because I was sure you would've said something about it."

"No, I didn't know."

"The police are going to keep the pregnancy quiet. The public will never know about it unless it comes out at a trial. I removed a few pictures of Tanya at the hospital in Santa Barbara. Everything else we have is on the discs. The FBI seemed very cooperative about releasing some information to you, which seems a little strange to me. I also included the pictures you obtained from that little girl in Los Gatos, a nice little piece of detective work I might add. I thought you'd like everything in one place. With any luck he's using one of the two remaining cars. Every police department in the state, hell, the whole country, has the information. They all want to catch him. Maybe this will be over quickly.

"Personally, my biggest worry is that he's headed back to Mexico or some other foreign country. I promise you, though, wherever he runs, we'll track him down."

McAllister had nothing to add.

"Apparently the Cobra showed her a short video of you and me having breakfast the day after she was taken. Remember the old man who bumped into you?"

McAllister's blood boiled and he could feel his face flush hot. "He really rubbed my nose in it. I'm going to remember all of this when I catch him."

"One last item and we're done. Every agency knows you're going after him and there seems to be a collective agreement to try to help you. You have to keep quiet about what I'm going to say next. Tomorrow you're going to get a phone call from Delmas Whitaker, a man well known in California law enforcement circles. Delmas is an absolute authority on the Cobra. Chasing the Cobra has been his full time job for some time. The authorities will use him to funnel any new leads to you. Listen closely when he calls. He's going to be the best friend you've ever had."

"He's got a full time job chasing the Cobra?"

"He's got as much skin in this as you do."

"Nobody could have as much in this as I do."

"Think about it. He does."

McAllister began to focus on the new challenge. "I don't remember how he got the name, Cobra?"

"He strikes silently and deadly. He made a career out of breaking into homes when the owners were asleep, then robbing his victims or worse. They never heard him until it was too late."

When the chief dropped Michael back at the station his hand disappeared into the catcher's mitt one last time.

"Thanks for your help with De Costa. If you ever need me, just call."

McAllister's mind was spinning with the new information as he walked back to Lucille. Tracy Carson was waiting beside the old Jag.

"We didn't get a chance for a lunch to talk shop. Are you going to have any time in the next few days?"

"No. I'm afraid I've got a full-time job ahead of me."

"Are you leaving town?"

"Probably but I won't know until tomorrow."

"Will you at least call the next time you're in town?"

"I promise I'll buy lunch if I come back this way."

Michael extended his hand but Stacy had a different idea, giving him a strong hug then turning away without another word.

His old friend from Tulsa, insomnia, returned for good that night. As he wrestled the bed sheets, Tanya's pregnancy was impossible to shake. Worst of all, he realized how hysterically happy her mother had been when she found out about the pregnancy and then how much worse it was to lose her. An image of Tanya swinging a table leg in an attempt to save her life kept running in an endless loop through his brain. Could a man named Delmas Whitaker possibly help him find the Cobra? McAllister had to believe he could, his only hope in an otherwise hopeless situation.

Chapter 52

The next morning McAllister noticed his clothes and personal belongings from Peter Stafford's house had been stacked neatly in the living room. His cell phone rang while he was trying to come up with a plan for breakfast.

"I'm listening."

"This is Delmas Whitaker. Can you talk?"

"You've got my undivided attention."

"I was the sheriff in Ventura County for almost twenty-five years but I'm retired now. The Cobra got his start down here in Ventura and Santa Barbara counties. I promised myself I'd catch him before I retired. I'm pretty pissed off I failed. I've collected every piece of information on every one of his cases over the years. I know more about him than anybody.

"A lot of the police were scared of the Cobra back in the old days. Too many of 'em didn't really want to try to catch up with him because they had wives and kids and pensions and who knows what. I've been told you're a man who isn't scared to go after him, a man who doesn't have attachments to a family or job holding him back, a man who doesn't care too much about risking his life. I need a man who could become obsessed with this case."

"Cut the bull shit. What do I do?"

"I want you to come to Ventura."

"I'll be there today. Should I call you on this number when I arrive?"

"You don't understand, son. I want you to move to Ventura. I have a plan that I'm pretty sure will snare the Cobra but it's going to take some time to set up. I've got to teach you all I know while we get ready."

"I can still be there today."

"Get down here and find a place to live. I want you to have a real address, phone, e-mail, everything. When you're ready, give me a call on this number. Don't be in a rush. I'm in this for the long haul. You better be, too."

"The chief said you had as much invested in this case as I do. Convince me."

"We can talk about that later. Get down here and get situated."

McAllister immediately entered Delmas in the contacts on his cell phone. One last piece of unfinished business remained before he left town.

Chapter 53

"Blue, Michael."

"What can I say? I'm so sorry about Tanya."

"I need to talk to you today if possible. What's convenient?"

"I'm covered up at work right now. Come by my place this evening, say seven?"

McAllister spent most of the day getting organized so he could head south to Ventura first thing in the morning. Lucille wouldn't carry much so he packed two soft bags of clothes and a back pack containing his computer, positioning the rest of his meager possessions near the back door, including his two guitars and an amp. Pausing in the bedroom, he picked up Tanya's pillow; still scented by her perfume and shampoo. He thought briefly about taking the pillow case with him but decided he was going to have a tough enough time keeping his sanity as it was. By evening everything was arranged.

Dusk shrouded the old Waldorf place when he fired up Lucille for the short drive to Blue's house. De Costa must have heard the Jag coming because he was at the garage door when Michael pulled up.

"Let's go upstairs where we can be comfortable. I've got a cold Diet Dr. Pepper for you."

McAllister had to smile at Blue's thoughtfulness. When they were settled Blue spoke first. "I'll never be able to thank you enough for helping me. At least I know what happened to my parents. I guess I'll learn to live with it."

"I didn't really do much on your father's case. The criminals took care of our job for us."

"You found them when I asked for your help. You kept us pointed in the right direction. I just want you to know how much I appreciate what you did for me. I'll never forget it. You won't take money so at least take my friendship. I'll always be here for you if you need anything."

Michael got down to business. "I want to say something to you face to face. When you first tried to hire me to find out who killed your parents, you asked me to bring them to you, not the police, because you wanted to take care of it yourself. I remember giving you a little lecture about being an officer of the court, right and wrong, all that crap. I said I obeyed the letter of the law at all times. I said I knew how you felt but I had to turn over anything I found to the police. Well, now I want to apologize."

"Apologize?"

"Yes, apologize. I didn't know how you felt." McAllister's voice cracked as he spat out the words. "I hadn't lost a family member like you had. Now, unfortunately, I do know how you felt. I just want to say I'm sorry for what I said to you."

"I still don't get it."

"I'm going after the man who killed Tanya. When I find him, I'm not planning to arrest him." The words hung in mid-air for a moment.

"You don't owe my any kind of an apology. If there's any way I can help you find him, please let me know. I have almost fifty full time employees in my company. We can bring a lot of power to bear if you need us."

"Thanks. Who knows? I may need your help one of these days." Michael was finished so he stood up to leave. "What's next for you now, Blue?"

"Believe it or not I'm going to Italy for a month to find a bride. I'm going to visit the old country so I can spend time with my relatives. They're lining up potential wives for me to interview. They say they've waited long enough."

"Tanya was pregnant."

Blue didn't verbally respond to his comment but the pain in his eyes told McAllister everything he needed to know, seeming to fully appreciate the loss of his last chance to have a family.

"What about you?"

"I'm heading to Ventura to work with a man there who supposedly can help me find Tanya's killer. It's probably going to take a while."

"So you're moving then?"

"Yes. I've been evicted from the old Waldorf place. Tanya's mom even got a restraining order against me. I guess I understand how she feels."

"What happened to Tanya wasn't your fault."

"She needs to blame someone for now. I don't mind if she uses me."

"What do you think will happen to the Waldorf mansion?"

"I'm sure her mother will sell it."

Blue paused, then asked a question that seemed to have been on his mind from the start. "Would you be offended if I tried to buy it?"

The idea caught McAllister off guard. "No. When I think about it, though, I guess it would make sense. After all, your great-grandmother is buried on the property. Your own blood built it. I think it would be fitting if you owned the property. Just don't mention my name during the negotiations."

"This will always be my parents' house. I think I need to have something that's mine. It's time for me to establish myself and my own family."

McAllister read him Tanya's mom's cell phone number, reminding him she probably wouldn't pick up at first but to be persistent. Suddenly one of Peter's quotes came to mind.

"What about the cars?"

"You mean the Jaguars?"

"They belonged to your family as well. I'm sure Tanya's mother will get rid of them. You might as well approach her with a package deal. You could return them all to the racing garage like they were so many years ago. It would be fitting."

As McAllister drove home he thought of the amazing symmetry of Valentino De Costa living at the old Waldorf mansion. The detective had already called a real estate agent before he went to Blue's place, who could help him find a place to live in Ventura.

His soul had grown darker and colder than the steel of the old Jaguar as they sliced their way through the fog on the drive back to the Waldorf mansion. As he drove the lessons his father had taught him ran through his mind. In every situation there was a right and wrong. Decisions were black and white. A career as a detective took it a step further. The police were in charge of protecting good from evil. Their job was to discern right from wrong.

Now his life was destined to finish in a grey area, somewhere between good and evil. Every day would be spent tracking down the Cobra, the man who had killed Tanya. Any means necessary, inside or outside the law, would be employed to achieve a successful result. No study groups or committees would be needed. No management team would be consulted. No questions would be asked about expenses, over-time or holidays. Mentally signing his name at the bottom of a deadly contract, McAllister prepared for his quest to find the Cobra.

The End

Michael McAllister Mystery Series:

Book 1 The Jaguar Conspiracy (2012)

Book 2 A Killer's Revenge (2014)

Book 3 Deadly Contract (coming soon)

Book 4 The Bugatti Affair (coming soon)

To keep up with activity on the Michael McAllister Mystery series join me on

Facebook: Paul.McNabb.5

Made in the USA
San Bernardino, CA
17 May 2015